Circlet of Gold

Hettie Aston

This is a work of fiction. Unless otherwise indicated, all the names, characters, businesses, places, events and incidents in this book are either the product of the author's imagination or used in a fictitious manner. Any resemblance to actual persons, living or dead, or actual events is purely coincidental.

Published by Hettie Aston
Publishing partner: Paragon Publishing, Rothersthorpe
First published 2020

© Hettie Aston 2020

The rights of Hettie Aston to be identified as the author of this work have been asserted by her in accordance with the Copyright, Designs and Patents Act of 1988.

All rights reserved; no part of this publication may be reproduced, stored in a retrieval system, or transmitted in any form or by any means, electronic, mechanical, photocopying, recording or otherwise without the prior written consent of the publisher or a licence permitting copying in the UK issued by the Copyright Licensing Agency Ltd. www.cla.co.uk

ISBN 978-1-78222-803-5

Book design, layout and production management by Into Print
www.intoprint.net
+44 (0)1604 832149

*To my husband and family.
Thank you all for your patience and encouragement
during the writing of the trilogy.*

Circlet of Gold

One

It was a Tuesday in May 1935, rather similar to any other Tuesday. I was holding a letter, fresh from the postman's hand, which had an air of officialdom about it. The brown envelope was addressed to Miss B. Dawson, Guardian of John Flitch; I quickly made the decision to wait to open it until John arrived home from school when we could read the letter together.

The previous day had been a national holiday in celebration of the Silver Jubilee anniversary of King George V and Queen Mary. A military parade marched through Ransington and the children had lined the streets waving their Union Jack flags.

Following the parade my aunt Vera and uncle Angus held a tea party at Iona House for our children and their friends; with plenty of party food which we had endeavoured to give a red, white and blue theme. We enjoyed games in the garden and it was considered by all to have made a welcome change from a usual Monday.

The triplets, Douglas, Caelan and Izzadora, were now almost five months old, all thriving and keeping us busy. Their mother Vera had recovered well from her caesarian section, thanks largely due to the care she had received at the Morgan Endowment hospital and from nurse Jean Fellows at home.

Mabel, our mother's help, looked after Claudette now 3 years and Rory 2 years but, with five children under the age of five and my two brothers now 8 years and almost 11 years, we acknowledged the need for more help.

"Remember your friend Evaleen, the one who was a nanny?" Vera asked me. "Do you think she might know someone looking for a post as nanny?"

"Not sure," was my reply. "I doubt she would want to return to Ransington, but I'll write and ask her if she knows of anyone."

The ringing of the telephone brought unwelcome news.

With characteristic decisiveness, Miss Starling, secretary to the headmaster at the boy's school, informed me that John had severe tummy pains and had been vomiting.

"I would appreciate immediate collection from school Miss Dawson for fear it could be contagious. John is here in my office. Are you able to come at once?"

I, of course, replied that I would collect John straight away.

Acute appendicitis was diagnosed by Dr Moshe Salmon, our family doctor, with urgent admission to hospital without delay. The Infirmary being the choice for emergencies that day.

Miss Newsome, the surgeon, with an entourage of medical students in tow, examined John and confirmed the diagnosis.

"Immediate surgery is necessary," she, with great alacrity, informed the students and myself.

"And why so?" she then addressed a scruffy looking undergraduate, sleepily loitering at the back of the group.

"The appendix may rupture or perforate, followed by sepsis and death" came the text book answer from the scruffy student, with untidy hair and shoes in need of a polish.

I felt my heart sink.

"Quite so, and not to put too fine a point on it we must now make haste," said Miss Newsome. "Your brother is young and healthy," she said, addressing me. "I do not envisage any problems." Glowing with confidence Miss Newsome swept out of the ward heading for the operating theatre; her clutch of medical students following behind. "One of you," I heard her loudly inform the group, "will be scrubbed up and assisting me in theatre."

The ward sister, Perdita Spinks, was a woman in her late twenties I would say. She was totally dedicated to her vocation of paediatric nursing, running the children's ward with kindness, compassion and rules. Her porcelain complexion and full pink mouth gave her an almost doll like face, spoilt only by a few premature frown lines above her peat brown eyes. Sister Spink's pencil slim figure carried her navy blue uniform well and with a starched frilly nurse's hat perching on top of her chestnut curls she looked the epitome of efficiency.

A dashing, handsome, doctor came to John's bedside, introducing himself as Dr Thistlethwaite, the anaesthetist.

"Does John suffer from any allergies, heart or chest problems?" he asked me, whilst listening to John's heart with a stethoscope.

I answered no and was asked to sign a consent form.

"Well John, I'll see you shortly," said the smiling Dr Thistlethwaite.

I couldn't help but notice that the white hospital coat he was wearing complemented his long, lean frame and bronzed complexion.

Going over to where Sister Spinks was sitting, he then perched on the edge of her desk and they had a conversation. I observed that Sister Spinks was smiling, blushing and indicating by her body language that whatever they were speaking about was of a personal nature, rather than work related. Judging by his body language I would say they were flirting.

John was taken to the operating theatre and, on leaving, I was asked to telephone the ward later in the day. I was then given a card on which were printed the strict visiting hours and information regarding who and how many visitors were allowed.

I then went to find a telephone to phone Iona House and tell Vera what was happening, after which it would be time to meet Alfie from school.

Walking towards the reception area of the hospital I followed behind two junior nurses; overhearing their conversation was unavoidable.

"He's asked her out for a date. Spinksy, that is," said nurse one.

"Never in the world!" exclaimed the second nurse, adding "Do you think she'll go?"

"Spect so, she's fancied him for ages," replied nurse one.

"Did you know he's been skiing?" said the second nurse.

"Skiing in *May!* Where do you suppose you can ski in May? Sun lamp more likely," replied nurse one.

Arm in arm they giggled their way down the corridor.

I wondered if Sister Spinks and Dr Thistlethwaite were aware of the interest the junior staff took in them.

Later that evening I called back to the Infirmary and enquired at the children's ward how John was progressing.

Visiting hour was now over so officially I was not allowed into the ward; however, a smiling Sister Spinks informed me that John had had his operation and there were no complications. She emphasised that visiting hours were strict and needed to be adhered to, then said, "You can pop and see him now for two minutes, just to reassure yourself. John will be with us for ten days and I can see you are anxious. Try not to worry we will look after him well."

John was sleeping and the nurses were settling the other children down for the night so I did only stay two minutes and I did feel reassured.

Visiting hours were indeed strict and limited to one hour each afternoon, two visitors only to each patient and no children allowed to visit.

A notice at the ward entrance clearly stated the visiting times followed by, and written in red, NO SWEETS OR CHOCOLATE ALLOWED and ALL FRUIT TO BE HANDED TO THE STAFF.

At visiting times we, the visitors, checked in and endured the 'bag search' by two nurses at the entrance to the ward; fruit was handed over to be shared by all the children. Clean nightwear and toiletries were allowed but definitely no contraband ie sweets or chocolate.

However, knowing that John was partial to a Fry's chocolate cream bar, my hat became a suitable hiding place and he the happy recipient.

Vera came to visit John, as did Stan and Mrs Scribbins; all brought treats hidden in their clothing.

Alfie, Claudette and Rory missed John and about three days following his operation Mabel took all three children into the small garden beside the children's ward.

Rory banged a drum, Claudette rattled a tambourine and Alfie helped Mabel hold up a banner which read, 'GET WELL SOON JOHN'. I helped him to stand on his bed and look out of the high Victorian window to wave. Sister Spinks tried to look disapproving but I caught a smile on her lips and warmth show in her eyes.

A quiet, pale-faced girl lay in the bed opposite John and I noticed she never had any visitors. A bed cradle supported the bedding which covered her legs and she used a pulley contraption to help her to move up the bed.

One day I asked John, "That girl never has any visitors, do you know why?"

His reply shocked me. "Her mam was a widow and she was killed when the tram hit them. They were crossing the road. Ivy, that's her name, has a broken leg, she's had an operation on it."

"Does she have any other relatives?" I enquired.

"Only her auntie, but she lives in Australia," John replied before lowering his voice and adding discreetly, "She's fourteen and she also likes Fry's chocolate cream bars."

This information, of course, necessitated me hiding two chocolate cream bars under my hat at each visiting time.

On John's tenth post operative day I was allowed to take him home to Iona House. Before leaving I met with the lady almoner, introduced myself and asked if it would be possible for me to visit Ivy following John's discharge from the hospital. She affirmed that I could and also thought it to be a good idea.

I asked Ivy if she would like me to visit and her beaming smile was all the answer I needed.

The short journey home was quite tiring for John so I

tucked him up on the sofa and we opened the official letter together. It read:-

Office of Education,
Town Hall,
Ransington.

Dear Miss Dawson,

I am pleased to inform you that your brother, John Flitch, has passed the scholarship entrance examination for the grammar school.
From September 1935, a place has been reserved for him at Ransington High School.
Please would you confirm acceptance of the placement, in writing, by June 1st, 1935.

Yours faithfully,

Elijah Somerton.
Director of Education.

We both agreed that I should write to Mr Somerton and accept the place for John at the grammar school.

2

The Nanny

A letter arrived for me from Evaleen.

56 Shapher Street
Huddersfield

May 30th, 1935

Dear Bettina,

Thank you for your letter. It is always good to hear your news and I hope your brother John is recovering from his appendectomy.
I am settled here and enjoy working in the hat shop. I doubt I will return to being a nanny.
I have an acquaintance, Doreen Kelly, who I happen to know is wanting to change her employer. She is a trained nanny so it might be worth contacting her.
Doreen's address is 6 Warfdon Buildings, Liverpool.
You didn't mention Stan in your last letter. Is it all off between you?
My brother John is married now and I'm walking out with a young man called Reginald. He works at the council offices.
Mam says to mention she is asking after you.
Love,
Evaleen xxx

Following discussion with Vera it was decided she would write to Doreen Kelly with a view to interviewing her for the post of nanny.

Stan's gardening business was developing fast and he had made the decision to rent premises and move the office from the tower room in Iona House to the new site. He also offered me the opportunity of working for him full time but I declined as I had other plans. My idea was to start my own business making exclusive underwear for the top end of the market.

John recovered his health well and was soon settled back at school and now looking forward to attending the grammar school in September.

I visited Ivy in hospital every few days and she told me that she would soon be having her fifteenth birthday and as her leg was better she would be leaving hospital.

"Leaving hospital," I said, "where will you go?"

"The lady almoner thinks I should go into service, perhaps in a big house, 'cause then I'll get me bed and board," she replied.

"How do you feel about that?" I asked.

"Not sure. Me leg's better now but I wouldn't know anybody, would I?" she answered.

"Well we'll just have to try to think of something," I said, without much confidence.

The 'something' turned out to be a job helping with domestic work at Iona House.

When I had explained to Vera that Ivy had no one in the world except her auntie in Australia, she said, "Bring her here, Mrs Scribbins and Mrs Handyside could do with an extra pair of hands. I only hope she likes children and the noise which goes with them."

"Is there any chance she could live in?" I asked.

"I don't see why not. That little bedroom at the back of the house might suit her. See what she thinks," Vera replied.

Ivy thought that to live at Iona House with a job would be perfect.

"Like landin' on me feet," she said. "Except I'm not chancin jumpin off anythin just yet, me leg's only just better."

Adam, my fiancé and love of my life, would be working in America at least until September. His letters to me were factual, telling of life there where everything sounded bigger, better, faster and brasher than in England; whereas I told him about the family. We both wrote of our longing for each other and of his return when, together, we could plan our wedding.

Our family doctors Moshe and Anna were now married, as were Percy our chauffeur and Iris who had been a widow.

I often daydreamed of my own wedding to Adam. The venue, the dress, the flowers. In reality I was part of a busy household and the possibility of having a nanny to share the load was becoming increasingly attractive.

Doreen arrived for her interview by car, driven by a thin young man wearing spectacles whom she introduced as her cousin.

He waited for her in the car and I couldn't help but notice that she dressed in a manner somewhat unusual for a nanny. Nannies were usually more conservative with their outfits than the one worn for the interview by Doreen. The crimson red damask coat with white fur collar she was wearing seemed rather incongruous for a nanny, as did the matching lips and fingernails.

Vera conducted the interview in the morning room and I asked a few pre-arranged questions.

"Do you have any experience of looking after several young children at one time?" I asked.

"Oh yes," she replied, "twins in the last household."

"Do you have any interests or hobbies?" was my next question.

"Reading, I love reading and I go to church every Sunday," she replied.

Doreen then gave a brief resume of her experience which seemed extremely comprehensive for a young woman of twenty years, but her references were good.

Vera then asked her if she had any questions.

"Not really," Doreen replied, "except about my days off. Will I be working set days or flexible?"

Vera assured Doreen that flexible days off could be programmed in to her working week. It was arranged that the new nanny would live in and commence working at Iona House the following week.

Doreen was extremely capable and the triplets were soon scheduled into a routine of feeding, sleeping and play. However, by the third week in her care they seemed restless, irritable and not sleeping at night. Vera and I took it in turns to comfort whichever one was awake whilst Doreen either slept or went out.

Following a few discreet enquiries by Percy our chauffeur, who seemed to know everyone in Ransington, we discovered that she frequented a cocktail bar in town where she met, and picked up, men for sex. Our wide-eyed, fresh faced nanny had a second job – that of moonlighting as a prostitute. Her *so called* cousin was her pimp and he had rented a room in a local brothel to enable Doreen to ply her trade. We now understood why she was so tired during the day, encouraging the triplets to sleep for long periods in the afternoon, and why they were so wakeful at night.

Her successor to the post of nanny to the triplets was in response to an advertisement Vera placed in *The Lady* magazine. Nora lived more locally and arrived for her interview by train from Stockton-on-Tees.

Immaculately dressed in a brown linen two-piece she looked slender and calm with a pale blond chignon. Nora, who had good references, wrote copious notes during her interview whilst holding a rigid expressionless face throughout.

Nora's post as nanny did not last long as baby Izzadora took an instant dislike to her, which we hoped would lessen as they became more accustomed to each other. However, Vera found the new nanny's ritual of practising outdoor yoga every morning in her brassiere and knickers unacceptable. She had also been seen walking naked between her bedroom and the bathroom.

Mrs Scribbins was heard to comment to Mrs Handyside, "That Nora, she's one of them nudists, told me that 'erself."

"Nudist, nudist, I've never heard the like. Bit bloody cold in the winter," Mrs Handyside said.

"Well, she prefers the word '*naturist*'. Must be nice not 'avin to think what to wear every day," said Mrs Scribbins.

"Well, I hope you're not going all naturist on us Mrs Scribbins. Mind if you do remember to bring a towel to put on the chair afore you sit down."

"Me naturist, not bloody likely. Imagine it, I could get me tits caught in the mangle on wash day," Mrs Scribbins said.

"Aye and a bit dangerous that would be and don't think I'd be sending my Stan round to rescue you," was Mrs Handyside's response.

This made them both crease up with laughter but did not solve the problem of the need for more help with the triplets.

Gwendoline, the third nanny, was a buxom blond girl with pouting full lips and a propensity for laughing uproariously at nothing in particular. Although she was excellent with the triplets, she had the unfortunate habit of going through pockets, dishes, purses and Mrs Handyside's tin of cash for the tradesmen which caused her employment with us to be very short lived.

Vera said in a frustrated tone of voice, "I'm at my wit's end. Who would have thought finding a nanny would be so difficult?"

"How's this for an idea?" I suggested. "Promote Mabel to nanny and give Ivy the job of mother's help."

Mabel and Ivy soon settled into their respective new roles bringing peace and harmony back to Iona House.

3

Oh Dear!

August 1935 brought with it a heatwave. With John, Alfie and Pip in my little Morris Minor we headed to the village of Little Laxlet for a visit to my aunt Agatha and her partner Francene, or Frank as she preferred to be called. Frank was a pharmacist at the chemist shop in Burside, the nearest market town to Little Laxlet.

As we drove out of Ransington the countryside beckoned. Fields and hedgerows replaced rows of terraced houses which backed onto more rows of houses separated only by cobbled back lanes.

Nearing Little Laxlet we noticed construction work underway about three miles from the village.

"That'll be the new airfield," John said. "A lad at school says his dad works there now."

I had heard rumours about the defence of Britain being improved due to Adolf Hitler, Fuerher of Germany, increasing his military capability and the possibility that he may wish to impose his rule on others. Another war was a fearful prospect; so much so that it was a topic rarely spoken about.

Little Laxlet looked as pretty as ever in the summer sunshine. The village green with its beech tree and telephone box, stone cottages and houses all with walled gardens, resplendent with flowers, basking in the sun.

Aunt Agatha and Frank lived in Providence House together, an arrangement which suited them. I jointly owned the house with Agatha, bequeathed to us by my grand parents who were her parents.

Providence House looked beautiful, with roses and honeysuckle cascading over the front porch. I inhaled the wonderful perfume whilst walking up the stone path, thinking that it seemed unbelievable that this lovely house had been so damaged by fire only two years before.

Agatha's welcome was warm but I noticed a blotchiness about her face and her eyes were red with crying.

John and Alfie went out to play with friends in the village and, over a cup of tea, Agatha opened her heart to me.

"It's Frank, we've split up. She's left me," Agatha spluttered through her tears.

"No I can't believe it," I commented, "you seemed so happy together."

"I know," sobbed Agatha, "but her parents called unexpectedly one day and caught us in bed together, making love in the studio."

"Oh dear, how embarrassing for you both," I remarked.

"Poor Frank. They just walked in, then her dad went into a fury," Agatha said. "He was shouting 'in flagrante, in flagrante' whilst pulling poor Frank out of the bed."

"How awful," I said.

"Oh it was. Frank was naked and her horrible father struck her across the back with his walking stick. 'Get dressed immediately' he shouted at her. 'this is not natural it's disgusting. Your mother and I will wait in the car and hurry up' Frank tried to protest but her mother just stood there like a frightened rabbit and he, the father, went on with his awful shouting, 'you're a disgrace the pair of you, it's not natural, a disgrace. We'll be in the car Francene and be quick I haven't got all day.' Then they left," Agatha said.

"Did Frank say anything?" I asked.

"No, other than I'm sorry Agatha, I'll write."

"And did she?"

"Yes. I received a letter signed, 'from Francene' explaining that her father lived by a strict moral code and that her mother was afraid of him. Sad as she was, our relationship had to end and if I would pack her things she would arrange for a van to collect them."

Agatha was wailing and sobbing, totally grief stricken at having lost the woman whom she loved dearly.

"They harangued Frank, harangued her, she had no choice," Agatha sobbed.

'There is always a choice', were my thoughts, but I declined to voice them.

"Oh dear, perhaps it will all blow over and Frank will come back" is what I did say, not quite knowing which words of comfort to offer.

I handed Agatha a clean, dry handkerchief which only resulted in causing her to wail more, becoming inconsolable.

Between sobs she told me that this was unlikely as Frank now had a boyfriend.

"A boyfriend, that was quick, are you sure?" I asked.

"Yes, he's a doctor she met at a pharmaceutical conference and I'm sure she's only going out with him to please her parents."

I held Agatha close as she cried into my shoulder, distraught with grief having lost her lover, Francene.

"Cooee – cooee," called Hilda who had been my next

door neighbour when I lived in Groat Cottage.

"Cooee," she called again, popping her head around the kitchen door."I saw your car Bettina. How are you, are you staying for long, where are the boys, what's wrong Agatha?" all in on breath.

Agatha pushed her damp hair off her forehead and made an attempt to compose herself.

"Cooee – cooee," called a second voice. It was Mrs Davis."I saw your car Bettina, how are you, lovely to see you, you look grand, I'll put the kettle on," she said, filling the kettle from the tap.

"Hello, hello," Ada yelled as she walked into the kitchen wearing a blue checked gingham skirt and a white cotton blouse.Her lustrous dark hair cascaded around her shoulders and I knew she was bringing news.

Agatha, now looking a little less distressed, began to explain to Hilda, Mrs Davis and Ada, who were all aware of her lesbian relationship, why she was so upset.

Over our cuppa we all agreed that marriage for Frank would be a terrible mistake as she had once told Agatha that to have sex with a man would be unthinkable.

"I've broken up with Bertie," Ada said. "Given him the ring back, the wedding is off."

"WHAT!" was my incredulous response. "You had such plans."

"Yes, well that didn't include having to listen to him boring me to death and falling asleep all the time. As for that bathroom of his, he could do with having a bath in it more often."

I weighed up my next question carefully, saying, "So you can't see yourself as Mrs Dixon then?"

"Not fucking likely, he's just looking for a skivvy. It's off. Definitely off," Ada replied.

"Have you heard about the cricket match?" asked Mrs Davis, " On the green next Sunday. Simon Blackwood's organising it and he said to ask if John and Alfie can be on his team."

"They can as far as I'm concerned, I'll ask them," I said. "By the way I noticed that the new airfield is well under way. Lots of construction going on as we passed on our way here."

"Yes," Ada said, "The workers drink here in the village at 'The Shoulder of Mutton'. Jim's doing a roaring trade."

"There's a dance on in the officers mess at the camp tonight," she continued. "Do you fancy going?"

I detected that Ada was not upset by her broken engagement, in fact she looked radiant. Agatha agreed to look after the boys, who came home excited at the prospect of a cricket match the following day. So it was agreed that Ada and I would go to the dance that night in the officers' mess.

A young soldier called Max was selling tickets on the door. Ada seemed to know him so we benefited from his 'special offer'.

"Two for the price of one," he said with a wink.

"Thanks," said Ada, shooting him a big smile.

"He's a friend of me brother-in-law Sammy," whispered Ada to me as we went in.

The dance hall smelled of grease and beer. A thick pall of cigarette smoke hung in the air, however the band sounded good.

The drinks were also two for the price of one. I was definitely gaining the impression that Ada had a lot of friends.

We found a table in a quiet corner which meant we could catch up with each others news.

Adam would be in America until September so I only had his letters to talk about which was a good thing as Ada was anxious to tell me about her break up with Bertie.

"We have an incompatibility," she said emphatically, "I wrote to that agony aunt in 'Woman and Home' and that's what she told me. An incompatibility."

"In what way?" I naively asked.

"Well I might as well get straight to the point and you are me best friend, basically I like a good shag and he doesn't. Simple as that," she replied.

"But I thought you were saving yourself for your wedding night," was my response.

"I was but then I changed me mind. So I put him to the test," Ada said.

"A test, what kind of test?" was my intrigued enquiry.

"I waited for a full moon and we went for a walk beside the river. I'd left me knickers off deliberately. Fresh air round your muffy Bettina, it's a real turn on. Well we're sitting there on the grass looking at the moon, very romantic it was. Then we kissed. He likes that I can tell. So I unbuttoned his flies, which he also likes," Ada said, sipping her shandy.

I began to wonder where this romantic story was going.

"It's all hotting up nicely," Ada said, "he's unbuttoning the front of me dress. Likes to squeeze me tits he does. I had his cock in me hand, huge and red hot it was, and I said to him all romantic and sexy like, 'shall we have a fuck'?"

I took a gulp of my shandy thinking, 'I'm pleased we found a quiet corner.'

Ada continued, "No, no, no he shouts. What do you

mean, no, no, no I asked him. I can't, I won't, don't want to he says, all upset he was. Kills the moment I can tell you. The romantic moonlit shag I was hoping for turned out to be a real disappointment. Me raring to go and well up for it and his dick now just hanging there. I've seen more life in a line of washing on a foggy day."

"That's very odd," I said. "Most men wouldn't need to be asked twice. Very odd indeed."

"Odd!" Ada exclaimed, "Not as odd as his fucking mother. Religious she was, reckoned she'd seen the light. It was her told him the facts of life and you're not going to believe this Bettina but he still thinks a baby is brought by a stork."

"Are you serious Ada? He's a farmer, he should know the facts of life," I said, astounded.

"Anyway it's even more peculiar than that, Bertie slept with his mother until he was seventeen years old. Now is that normal?" she asked.

"Why?" was my next question.

"In case he needed anything in the night. That's what she told him. Personally I think it was because she didn't want to have sex with Bertie's dad. There was only ever one child," Ada explained.

We sat in silence for a few moments watching the dancing.

"They sang hymns together in bed Bertie and his mother," Ada said.

This story was becoming weirder by the minute.

Ada went on, "Yes hymns and she played old anthems to him on her harmonium in the bedroom."

"So no nice bedtime stories for poor Bertie then," I said, starting to feel sorry for him.

"No, she really messed with his head. Told him sex was

normal, even essential for animals, but not for humans. She told him he was never to put his 'todger', as she called it, into any 'lady parts' or he would die," Ada continued. "Fucking mad she was."

"Perhaps you could try again," I tentatively enquired.

"We have, and it's always the same," Ada replied.

"That's a shame," I consoled.

"I know and I really like his dad. Would have made a great father-in-law.

"It just seems so sad to me," I said.

"I know," said Ada, "so now I'm on the look out. Plenty more fish in the sea."

A good looking, pipe smoking officer asked Ada to dance and I was left alone and wishing Adam wasn't thousands of miles away.

A young man with a ginger moustache asked me to dance and Ada and I enjoyed the remainder of the evening.

At about 11pm I said to Ada that I must go home to Providence House and asked would she like a lift back to the farm. She chose to stay on with the good looking officer who assured me that he would make sure Ada returned home safely.

Apparently she did, at around 4am; the good looking young officer having made up for the attributes Bertie lacked!

4

Silk

Lady Rachael Styles from The Manor, Little Laxlet, called at Providence House to discuss the cricket match which was scheduled to take place on the village green the following Sunday. Wearing a floral summer day dress with jacket to match, her straw hat decorated with roses shading her porcelain skin, which appeared to be unlined; she was undoubtedly still as beautiful as I'd read about in 'The Tatler'.

I estimated her age to be about seventy and she looked as cool as a cucumber, even on such a swelteringly hot day.

Little Laxlet would be playing a team from Burside; creating much interest in the village with bets being placed as to which team would win.

I offered Lady Rachael tea with home made cake and biscuits in the orangery, which she accepted.

"It's been so long since I've seen you and your boys Louisa, my how they have grown," she said, sipping her tea and accepting a biscuit.

"They certainly have," was my polite reply. "How are you and Sir Simeon keeping?"

"We are in the rudest of health thank you. In fact Simeon will be playing in the match on Sunday," she said, slipping a biscuit into her pocket.

"It should be good fun," I said. "Both John and Alfie are on the Little Laxlet team. I think we are putting on the cricketers tea here at Providence House as we are nearest to the green."

"Splendid, splendid," she said, "However, the real reason I called was to ask if you ever do any sewing my dear? I seem to recall that you have always been, and probably still are, extremely adept with the needle."

"I do, and it's a coincidence you should ask as the reason for my visit to Little Laxlet is to discuss with Agatha the sewing business we are planning to start," I answered.

"Oh, how interesting. Will it be dressmaking?" Lady Styles asked.

"Not exactly, we are planning to make exclusive silk and lace underwear for the high end of the market," was my answer.

"What a brilliant idea. I have several friends whose daughters are either in Germany or planning to go to Germany to 'finish'. They are débutantes and just love being over there. The music, the parties, the young men," she sighed.

"Do you think they would buy our silk cami-knickers and negligées? I asked.

"I'm certain their mother's would. The girls 'finish' in Germany or Austria and at the same time look for a rich husband; preferably one with a royal blood line," she said.

"But what about Hitler and his Nazi party?" I queried.

"Aristocrats are not in the least concerned. Their daughters are well looked after. Parties from morning 'till night, if you know what I mean," she replied, winking and nodding in a knowing way, before blowing her nose on the linen, lace-edged table napkin, which she then put in her pocket.

"The 'debs.' are always on the look out for the latest

fashion. What would you say to me putting out a few feelers for you and please Louisa would you call me Rachael?"

"Thank you Rachael, I would really appreciate it if you would," I replied, not correcting her in mistaking my name for that of my mother, or commenting on the biscuit and linen napkin which were now in her pocket.

This was the news I needed to spur me into action regarding the embryonic idea for a business.

That evening, when the boys had gone to bed, Agatha and I held our first meeting. We made copious notes and lists regarding fabrics, thread, ribbons, packaging etc. But mainly we discussed the importance of advertising and promoting the business.

The next day an appointment was made for the following week with Mr Hadleigh of Macclesfield who was a wholesaler of silk.

John and Alfie were excited about the cricket match and spent most of every day practising with Simon Blackwood and the other village boys on the green. The centre of the green was mown and there was much conversation about the wicket, the weather and the spin. I didn't even pretend to understand half of what they were talking about.

With help from Mrs Davis, Agatha and I made cakes, scones, sandwiches and of course there were slices of Mrs Davis's prize-winning fruit cake. The kitchen table at Providence House was heavily laden with food for the 'Cricketers Tea' which we covered with a clean bed sheet and took our deckchairs onto the green to watch the match.

Agatha seemed visibly less upset about her personal life and I was pleased the cricket match had taken her mind off Frank.

I found sitting with Pip and Sophie, watching the cricket, relaxing whilst piecing some fabric diamond shapes in readiness for my next quilt.

Agatha dozed under her straw sun hat; only to join in with the occasional ripple of gentle fluttering applause which denoted runs.

Little Laxlet were all out for 168 runs and did not win the cricket match; the score being 169 not out to the team from Burside, making them the deserved victors.

Over tea the conversation became competitive. It was suggested that the best lads from Burside and Little Laxlet would join together to form a country team. Angus would be asked to make up a town team from the workers at Landsdown Short iron and steel works in Ransington. If this could be arranged the cricket match between town and country would be on the last Sunday in August.

Over tea Lady Rachael told me she had spoken to several of her friends, all of whom thought the prospect of having high quality, bespoke underwear to be a fabulous idea. She also insisted on calling me Louisa and as she left the kitchen to use the facilities in the boot room Rachael struggled with opening the door – it was if she had forgotten such a simple task. After following her into the boot-room I felt concerned as I discovered she had left the taps running.

John and Alfie were not even remotely interested in accompanying Agatha and me to Macclesfield and were quite happy to stay in Little Laxlet with Hilda for the day.

We travelled by train, taking a taxi from the railway station to Hadleigh's Mill where we were met by Mr Hadleigh himself. He was a short serious man, dressed in a three piece checked tweed suit; perspiration stood in beads on his bald head and ran down his florid face.

By contrast, his daughter Charlie looked refreshingly cool, wearing blue cotton flared trousers and a matching blouse in a slightly paler shade of blue. Her dark, short, cropped hair and large, smiling brown eyes gave her a business like appearance but with warmth.

First we were shown small samples of silk in different weights in a limited variety of colours. White, rose pink and eau de nil.

When I explained to Mr Hadleigh that it was difficult to visualise a garment made up from such a modest sample he 'hummed and hawed' and couldn't understand why we were having a problem.

Charlie intervened, suggesting she took us around the area of the factory where the silk cloth was manufactured.

Her father was less than enthusiastic but eventually succumbed to Charlie's persuasion. Agatha and I were then taken on an escorted tour, firstly going through long narrow sheds which Charlie explained were the throwing sheds. We must have looked blank.

"It's where the workers twist the silk thread," she further explained. "The filament from the bobbins is given a full twist, including reeling and doubling."

We smiled at the piecers, winders and doublers attending to their reels and bobbins. All were women with the exception of one man who appeared to be in charge. Charlie explained the jobs and terminology as we went through the factory; to me it was a whole new language.

Speech became impossible in the weaving shed due to the noise of the looms. I noticed the workers were communicating in sign language and wondered if they could lip read.

The welcome quietness of the storage depot was comforting. It was where we could look at the lengths of silk fabric in a variety of colours and make our choices; the weight of the silk cloth being measured in mommes.

Charlie recommended white as always being popular for bridal underwear. Eau-de- nil and rose as being suitable for débutantes, black for the sophisticated woman and red for women of passion.

Our order of a bale each of Charmeuse and Crepe de chine, in white, rose and eau de nil (meaning colour of the Nile Charlie explained) was placed. This order, we were told, would be dispatched within the week and sent, by train and courier, to our door.

We now had a company account and should we require any further bales they could be ordered by telephone or letter.

Charlie then said, whilst ramming a cloche hat on top of her cropped hair, "I'm finished for the day now, would you be interested in having afternoon tea with me at the tearooms in the town centre?"

This seemed to be an excellent idea, especially as she told us she had a vehicle.

The vehicle was a motor-bike and side-car which transported us into town with Agatha sitting in the side-car and me riding pillion. Charlie rode with fearless speed, weaving in and out of the traffic, tooting the horn or shaking her fist at other drivers for most of the journey.

In the calm of the tearoom Charlie explained, "Father wanted a son to work alongside him in the business, then to take over in the fullness of time. He was definitely disappointed 'only to have a girl' and often told me so."

"That's shocking!" exclaimed Agatha.

"You seem most competent at what you do Charlie, we couldn't have managed without your help today," I said.

"Well, not that I want to blow my own trumpet or anything, but I'm as good as any lad. I know that business inside out," she said.

"Unlike us, we are complete novices," I said.

"Look," said Charlie, "Never undersell yourselves. You bought well today and your garments will fly off the shelves once you get going."

She then added, "What do you plan to do about advertising?"

"Yes we will need to advertise," I said.

"Any tips?" asked Agatha.

"It is always good to advertise but choose where you place your adverts with care. Magazines such as 'Vogue' are horrendously expensive, though 'The Lady' is good. Perhaps a few discreet business cards placed in milliners and hairdressers, printing is not too expensive.

We thanked Charlie and promised to keep in touch before heading for the railway-station with a box of French cream fancies for Hilda and the boys.

5

Cricket

An overcast sky heralded the Sunday morning of the town versus country cricket match. Due to consideration of safety to the public, a decision had been made that to hold the match in the park could be dangerous. The venue would be the Landsdown Short iron and steel works sports field.

The cricket tea would be in the sports clubhouse where the rat faced, bulging eyed chairman informed me that his wife, whom I noted had an aura of hopelessness about her, would be in charge of the food. The choice of bloater paste or brawn sandwiches, her speciality apparently, I felt did not bode well as a welcoming tea for visitors.

The majority of the Little Laxlet team arrived by coach, mostly wearing comfortable clothing. Sir Simeon Styles and his wife, Lady Rachael, travelled in their chauffeur driven Rolls Royce. He looked splendid in full cricketers 'whites' and wearing the purple velvet cap he'd won during his cricketing days at university. She, as always, looked cool and elegant wearing a cream linen two piece with a jade green straw hat. However I couldn't help but notice she was shaky on her feet, tripping twice, and taking Sir Simeon's arm to steady herself.

Ada, her dad, and several other folk from Burside and Little Laxlet arrived to support the country team. The townies had huge support from most of the workers of Lansdown Short.

The chairman of the sports club tossed a coin which the country team won and chose to bat first. Sir Simeon was the captain and decided that his best team member, Simon Blackwood would be first in to bat. Ian bowled for the townies and Simon was eventually bowled out for 37 runs which included a six.

"OWZAT!" shouted the townie crowd as the stumps fell.

Unsure as to whether I was supporting the town or country team I applauded Simon for a good innings.

Angus took over the bowling and the next two batsmen did well, scoring over 50 runs before one of them was caught out.

Sir Simeon Styles was fourth man in to bat and the bowler now changed to Digby Hanson, one of the managers from the works. Digby was a renowned, local, fast bowler and, as Simeon had won caps for his cricket, Angus as townie captain, decided a strong fast bowler was required. The first bowl was indeed fast but Sir Simeon hit it straight on and scored three runs. Digby, polishing the ball on his trousers then rubbing spittle onto it to make it spin, walked several paces back. He then ran, full speed at the crease and, with a straight arm, launched a fast ball down the pitch. It was a bouncer and how it did bounce, hitting Sir Simeon Styles hard on the side of his head.

He fell to the ground. Dr Moshe Salmon ran on to the pitch where Simeon lay unconscious. The country team and supporters gathered around their captain.

"Is he breathing?" Ada asked.

"I'll call an ambulance," shouted the chairman, running into the clubhouse.

There was no need, Sir Simeon Styles was dead.

I tried to comfort Lady Styles who was weeping.

"Do you have a sixpence?" she asked.

"Yes I do," I answered, perplexed as to why she would need a sixpence having just witnessed her husband, literally, drop down dead.

"You see, it's my suspender," she said.

"Your suspender?" I repeated.

"Yes, the little rubber button has dropped off one suspender and I feel so unsafe without all eight fastened. I find that in an emergency a sixpence makes a good substitute. This is an emergency isn't it?" was her explanation followed by a question.

"Yes Rachael it is. We'll find you a sixpence and I'll take you home," I said, gently shepherding her towards the car.

Ada and I travelled with Lady Rachael, chauffeured in the Rolls Royce, back to The Manor House at Little Laxlet.

Her maid Una was mending a hat when we arrived and I explained the situation.

Una said, "I have the telephone number of her Ladyship's sister, she lives in Devon."

Ada and I stayed the night with Lady Rachael who did have moments of lucidity but mostly rambled in an incoherent way. She was numb with shock following the accident and sudden death of Sir Simeon and remained so for the rest of her life. Her dementia progressed rapidly and eventually she went to live with her sister. The impressive Manor House, dating back in parts to the 15th century was now empty and locked.

*

A sunny September morning and a letter arrived from Bonny saying she would be back in Ransington for two weeks holiday and could we meet up. I had missed her since she had gone to the Royal Victoria Infirmary, Newcastle-upon-Tyne, for her nurse training. Her letter said that, although she was enjoying the work, she was looking forward to a break, especially her feet which, at the end of a shift, were always 'killing her'.

The boys were now back at school following the summer holidays. John was at the grammar school and Alfie at his old school where he had many friends.

Bonny and I met for lunch in the restaurant of the department store. I had decided that, as I knew nurses' pay was poor, lunch would be my treat. However, she had a voucher for 'lunch for two' which was a lovely surprise.

"I've just been working nights on the ward where everyone has their own room and, of course, it's more expensive; there are some very affluent patients, 'Privates' we call them," she said.

"Anyone famous?" I enquired.

"Not really, just rolling in money. They often give us presents. Vouchers for the pictures, hairdressers and restaurants mostly. Oh, and sometimes a box of chocolates," she said.

"Sounds as though they appreciate you nurses," I said.

"I think they do. Nurses have even been known to have a romance with a patient, although it's frowned upon."

"Are you having a romance?" I asked.

"No. I'm either too busy working or studying to have a love life. Tell me about your Adam. I don't even know what he looks like," she said.

"I'd forgotten you haven't met Adam," I said. "Well he's about five foot ten, so not too tall, brown eyes and hair, very good looking and an amazingly good dancer. He is in America studying law at Harvard but we write to each other regularly"

"He sounds gorgeous. Is he 'the one'?" she asked.

"Yes he truly is. Adam proposed by telephone on New Years Eve so we are engaged I suppose, but no wedding plans as yet," I said.

"When is he coming home?"

"Later this month and I just can't wait to see him again," I replied.

Our lunch of braised beef with vegetables was delicious, as were the apple tart and coffee to follow.

"Did you know that my aunt Agatha and Frank have split up?" I asked.

"No I didn't. I don't know your aunt well but isn't she the one who had a girlfriend?" Bonny asked.

"She is. They were so happy together but Frank's parents found out and were horrified that their daughter should be in a same sex relationship," I said.

"What a shame. I know a few nurses who are lesbians but they don't broadcast the fact," she said.

"Frank is now going out with a doctor she met at a conference. A Dr Thistlethwaite, I wonder if he's the same one I met when John had his appendix out," I said, adding, "Mary who is the telephonist at Burside police station told Ada that was his name."

"Thistlethwaite, not a common name," Bonny said, "I know a Dr Spencer Thistlethwaite but he's engaged to a nurse in my crowd. He could have a brother or cousin who is in medicine I suppose. Medical careers often run in families."

"That could explain it," I said. "Shall we go to the pictures one night?"

"Yes, what's on?"

"Top Hat, with Fred Astaire and Ginger Rogers is on at the Roxy, do you fancy that?"

"Sounds great. After this holiday I'm seconded to the Morgan Endowment hospital for my theatre training so I can live at home for a month. Believe me that will make a change from the nurses home and that old battleaxe of a home sister," Bonny said.

"Good, we can see more of each other. You must come over to Iona House. Vera would love you to meet the triplets and Claudette and Rory have really grown since you last saw them."

"Yes and I'd love to meet Adam when he returns," she said.

I received a letter from Adam and sat in the morning room in Iona House to read it. The letter told me he would be home on September 22nd. My constant dreaming of this day would shortly come to fruition, so why did I feel panic stricken?

Pip who always detected my mood, came over to me and jumped onto my lap. Stroking her calmed me; her beautiful amber, almond shaped eyes had a look as if to say, 'don't worry – it'll be fine'. I thought it was such a long time since I'd seen Adam I couldn't help wondering if things would be the same between us.

Bonny and Phyllis helped to calm me down before I went to meet Adam.

Wearing a burgundy coloured wool skirt and cream twin set which Phyllis had helped me choose. My gold locket with a picture of mam inside, burgundy shoes and handbag completed my ensemble; I waited with Pip, her lead firmly in my hand, on platform 3 at Ransington railway station for the 15:45 from London. Butterflies of excitement could scarcely be contained.

As the steam and the crowds cleared our eyes met, we ran towards each other, Adam dropped his suitcase and enfolded me in his arms. Our lips crushed in a long, passionate kiss, a kiss we had both longed for, for over a year. We had so much to discuss, a wedding to arrange, our future together; it was wonderful to have him home.

"Iona House is even busier than before you left" I told him as we drove there in my little Morris Minor, Pip sitting on Adam's lap. "Five children under five and the two boys."

"So you tell me in your letters. That is why I've planned a weekend away for us, just the two of us, how does that sound?" Adam said.

'Wonderful' is what I thought whilst saying, "but what about the boys?"

"All organised," said Adam. "I've arranged with Eliza Jane that we drop them off at High Stones. Then you and I head off to an hotel on the coast in Northumberland. I've booked us a room overlooking the castle and we will be near the sea."

"Do they take dogs?" I asked, glancing at Pip.

"Of course they do," Adam said, laughing as we arrived at Iona House.

A moment of quiet. Sitting in my little car we kissed again, then again. Our kisses deepening; a delight which was indescribably exquisite.

Handing me a small box Adam said, "I've brought you a gift."

I had an inkling of what it might be but was totally unprepared for the sight of a magnificent large emerald surrounded by diamonds. This was my engagement ring which Adam placed on my finger whilst telling me that the emerald was Columbian and the ring had been especially made for me.

He looked so at ease and strong whereas, to me, I seemed gauche and tense. I suspected it was because I hadn't seen him for so long.

"It's a beautiful ring," I said, stating the obvious.

"I bought the emerald in Columbia when I was there on business for Nick and a jewellers called Tiffany's in New York made it. It suits you perfectly," he said.

"New York, yes I recall you mentioned in one of your letters that you were there."

For a moment we sat in silence, then I said. "Thank you, we have so much to talk about."

"Indeed we do, and a wedding to arrange," Adam said, his eyes shining with love.

My heart soared, I stroked his lips and strong jaw line then we kissed again.

"Now," I said, "I don't intend to appear melodramatic but there are a lot of people waiting to welcome you home, so prepare yourself."

I need not have worried. Adam seemed more confident than ever since his stay in America and linking my arm through his we went into Iona House with Pip leading the way.

6

The Romantic Weekend

John and Alfie were excited to be staying with aunt Eliza Jane at High Stones, her fabulous Art Deco house with its indoor swimming pool.

On arrival my great aunt and her daughters, Winnie and Gladys, all admired my emerald and diamond engagement ring and had many questions about wedding plans.

The boys promised to be on their best behaviour at all times and not to go near the swimming pool unless accompanied by an adult.

Adam, Pip and I called in at the mining village of Denstag, the Rutherford's family home, to tell them of our engagement and forthcoming wedding. Their welcome was warm and loving; the thought of becoming part of this close family made my spirits sore.

"I'm taking Bettina to the Northumberland coast for a weekend away by the sea," Adam told his family.

"That sounds a perfect way to celebrate your engagement. Where will you be staying?" his mother, Mrs Rutherford, asked.

"It's a secret so all I can say is that we will be staying in an hotel and there is a castle," he answered.

"Oh, the coastline is beautiful there, it'll be just lovely by the sea," Mrs Rutherford said.

Adam's cousin Jenny called in, squealing with excitement

at the news of our engagement and full of admiration for the ring.

The Rutherford family were, without exception, eager to hear about a wedding date and disappointed that, as yet, it had not been arranged.

The sunset was stunning as we journeyed to our hotel in Bamburgh. A sky, breathtakingly beautiful, of reds, orange and pink hues streaked across the horizon beyond the Cheviot Hills.

It quickly became apparent that Adam and I would be sharing a bedroom, albeit a large one overlooking the castle, with a double bed and another bed which was a single. The room also had an en suite bathroom which we took in turns to use before we changed for dinner.

I wore a navy blue, light weight, woollen dress and Adam looked handsome in his grey double breasted suit and white shirt. I noticed he wore the blue paisley patterned silk tie I had sent to America for his birthday.

Over dinner, in the formal dining room of the hotel, Adam told me about America and the prospect of a new job with Nick Van der Linden.

"America, a new job. Where in America?" I asked.

"Chicago, I'll be working in Nick's law department, starting next year, January 1936," Adam said.

I felt stunned, as though I'd been kicked.

"But that means you'll be going away from me again," I said, trying to keep emotion out of my voice.

"Not if you come with me," was his reply.

Taken completely by surprise as I had not anticipated, for one moment, going to America, I said, "but what about the boys?"

"The boys?" Adam said. "I hadn't realised they came as part of the engagement and wedding plans. We'll have to give it some thought."

An awkward silence came between us – it was as though a bombshell had been dropped.

During dinner I noticed a couple, sitting not too far from our table; they were having an argument.

The man sat with his back to me, however I could see and hear the woman quite clearly; she wore a smart black chiffon beaded dress and seemed distressed.

"You utter bastard," shouted this pretty woman whom I noticed wore a red rose in her black wavy hair and her lips resembled a red heart.

"Keep your voice down Belinda," I heard the man say.

"You are so mean, so not nice," she said loudly.

I then heard him calmly say, "We are here to have a relaxing weekend. Your mother has the baby. Can't we just enjoy ourselves for once, just the two of us?"

"THE TWO OF US!" she shrieked, "The two of us, don't make me laugh. There are at least two more that I know of."

The woman stood up and grabbed the water jug, the contents of which she attempted to throw over her companion; failing to do so as he grabbed her arm.

"BASTARD, BASTARD!" she shrieked, wrenching her arm free then running out of the dining room. Her black designer dress now soaked with water and her face now streaming with tears.

The man, aware that he had the attention of all the diners, slowly rose from his chair, turned and left the room. I recognised him; it was Dr Thistlethwaite.

We decided to go for a walk after dinner and Adam went up to our room for Pip and my jacket.

As I waited in the reception area Dr Thistlethwaite and his wife came out of the bar and walked towards the lift. Mrs Thistlethwaite had changed into a different black dress, still with the red rose in her hair which matched her clutch bag. She swayed and tottered on her red high heels, clinging to his arm and announcing to all in the vicinity what a shit and a bastard he was – she appeared to be drunk.

Dr Spencer Thistlethwaite and his wife, Belinda, were spending a weekend by the sea in celebration of three years of marriage. A marriage he felt he had been forced into as he was almost certain she had initially feigned pregnancy to entrap him; followed by an actual pregnancy resulting in the birth of a child.

As we walked on the beach with Pip I told Adam who Dr Thistlethwaite was and that I recognised him from the Infirmary as he was the doctor who had administered John's anaesthetic. Adam seemed more interested to discuss our future together but how could I tell him that I was not prepared to leave the boys to go and live in America.

"You are very quiet," Adam said, "What's troubling you?"

Coming straight to the point I said, "Well I don't think I can just leave John and Alfie and go to live in America. They don't have anyone else. Their father is still in prison and Mrs Flitch, well I have no idea where she is. Neither of them ever contact the boys."

We walked on, only the sound of the waves broke the silence.

"Also I have plans to start a business with Agatha, we've ordered bales of silk from Macclesfield," I said.

Adam said he understood my point of view but I could detect disappointment in his voice.

"I was hoping we could be married as soon as possible, even by special licence," he said.

I remained quiet, we just kept walking.

"It's going to be a long engagement then," he said.

We walked in companionable silence, both feeling sad. As we arrived back at the hotel a cloud slipped across the face of the moon.

An ambulance stood at the entrance of the hotel. I recognised the patient being carried to it on a stretcher as Mrs Thistlethwaite; looking ill and no longer wearing the red rose in her hair. Deathly pale, she was driven away in the ambulance with the emergency bell ringing.

Dr Thistlethwaite had told the ambulance drivers he would follow on to the hospital after he had made a quick telephone call.

"Shall we have a nightcap?" Adam asked me.

"Good idea," I answered, thinking that if we could talk some more he might come to better understand my viewpoint.

"I'll just take Pip upstairs to our room and find my wallet," Adam said.

I sat down to wait for him in the reception area not realising my chair was beside the glass telephone kiosk.

Dr Thistlethwaite entered the telephone kiosk, which I don't think he was aware was not soundproof, and made a call.

"The room is booked," he said. "I have an emergency call at the local hospital here but should be back by 11pm. I'm longing to see you my darling. If I'm not in the foyer when you arrive just wait, I shouldn't be long. Must go. Love you."

He then left the hotel, I presumed, to drive to the local hospital.

Unbeknown to us and while we were walking, Mrs Thislethwaite had, on returning to their bedroom, become hysterical, screaming at her husband and throwing hotel property at him. A small vase was hurled at his head; missing the target but smashing into the bathroom mirror.

"You're a philanderin bastard. Fuck anythin with a pulse," she shouted in her drunken state.

"Keep calm darling. Yours nerves are kicking in, that's all," he said.

"*NERVES, NERVES, IT'S NO BLOODY WONDER MARRIED TO YOU. YOU, YOU BASTARD!*" she screamed at him.

"Why not take one of your tablets – it might soothe you?" he said, whilst thinking. 'It might shut the bitch up' and offering her a small bottle containing ten nembutal tablets.

On his return from the bathroom with a glass of water he witnessed his wife take one tablet with a drink of the water. She seemed calmer and began to undress then suddenly, and without warning, collapsed onto the bed. Dr Thistlethwaite then noticed that the small bottle was now empty and realised that his wife must have taken all the nembutal tablets. He made the decision not to rush but took his time clearing up the broken glass in the bathroom and tidied the bedroom. After about twenty minutes he telephoned reception and asked the manager to call for an emergency ambulance as his wife needed to go to the hospital without delay.

The lounge bar area of the hotel was furnished with overstuffed sofas and armchairs, the occupants of which were enjoying listening to the pianist play gentle tunes from the musical theatre. Conversation between the guests was civil and subdued, the ladies wore exclusive gowns and expensive perfume; the majority of the men were smoking.

Adam and I went into the lounge bar for a nightcap but the conversation we had regarding America and the boys had put a dampener on the evening.

Our conversation turned to discussing family and the weather; not subjects either of us had planned for our romantic weekend.

I did mention the telephone call I had overheard but Adam wasn't interested.

At 11pm we gave up trying to keep the conversation going and decided to go to bed. As we walked through the foyer of the hotel who should be sitting waiting but Sister Perdita Spinks.

Dr Thistlethwaite, who had stayed at the hospital just long enough for his wife to have her stomach pumped out, came rushing in through the main front door and ran towards Perdita; they embraced then, arm in arm, walked towards the lift. I noticed the two receptionists behind the desk exchange a knowing look, then shake their heads.

In the Thistlethwaite hotel bedroom, now immaculate and free from broken glass, the two lovers did not hesitate to rip off each others clothes before slipping, naked, between the sheets. Dr Thistlethwaite ran his hands over Perdita's svelte thighs whilst she caressed his face. Perdita loved the sensation of his lips on hers and as they kissed, a pulverising open mouthed kiss, tongues exploring, she felt love for him; a love which almost engulfed her.

His hands caressed her breasts and pert pink nipples; then, moving to her pubic area caressed her inner thighs and he knew, from experience, that this virgin was ready for him, which she was; her legs already parted and willing.

Without hesitation he entered her; rather brutally. Perdita's first experience of sex was not quite as joyful as she had hoped. However she was blindly in love with this charming, handsome man, whom she thought was single, so when they made love again about an hour later he did not rush and she experienced the delight of her first ever orgasm.

The red rose which had been in his wife's hair lay discarded in the waste paper basket!

Adam and I did not share the double bed in our beautiful hotel bedroom with a view of the castle. We had reached an impasse in our conversation which spoilt the whole mood of, what should have been, a romantic weekend. He slept in the single bed.

The following morning we checked out immediately after breakfast. As we were about to leave the hotel Dr Thistlthwaite and Perdita emerged from the lift, heading towards the dining room. She was flushed, I suspected from pre breakfast sex and they both looked relaxed and happy, unlike Mrs Thistlethwaite who was recovering in hospital and whose suspicions about her husband were absolutely correct.

Adam decided to spend some time with his parents so I dropped him off in Denstag before motoring to Gosforth to collect John and Alfie. Aunt Eliza Jane must have sensed my sadness and suggested a chat over a cup of tea and a slice of her orange cake.

I told her about Adam's suggestion that I go to live in America with him and that we should marry straight away by special licence. The weekend had not been a happy one for either of us and I felt better just talking to my aunt who listened and seemed unsurprised.

"Well," she said, "true love never runs smoothly, and I do believe it *is* true love. You need to get to know each other again. Just give it time."

7

The Circus

In early October a letter arrived for me from Ada.

> *Rookery Farm,*
> *Little Laxlet.*
>
> *3rd October, 1935.*
>
> *Dear Bettina,*
>
> *The circus is coming to Burside and I have four tickets. Why don't you bring the boys and we can all go together this next Saturday afternoon.*
> *By the way you won't believe it, Emrys Davis has asked me out for a date.*
> *I've waited ages for him to ask, so now I'm playing hard to get. I told him I'd think about it. Mind you, I'll watch my P's and Q's when we do go out!!*
> *Let me know about the circus.*
>
> *Love,*
>
> *Ada. xxxxx*
>
> *p.s. A rep promoting the circus gave me the tickets in return for putting up a poster in my aunty's shop. He wanted me to put it in the window of the police station but I told him that wasn't*

allowed so I'd put it in the window of my aunty's shop. I know I don't have an aunty with a shop but I did hang the poster in the police station bog and the main thing is we now have four tickets.

John and Alfie were keen to go to the circus; me, less so as I hated the idea of animals being caged and trained with whips.

As we approached the big top the boys became more excited. Surrounding the huge red and white striped tent were side shows, roundabouts, a waltzer and a helter-skelter; in other words, a fair.

The show people were shouting encouragement at the crowds to come and buy the experiences on offer. A two headed sheep and the bearded lady were just two of the attractions.

I promised the boys that we would look at the fair after we had been to the circus.

A fanfare of trumpets heralded into the ring the jovial ringmaster; he wore a red top hat and matching tail coat. Bowing to the audience and shouting in an alarmingly loud voice he introduced the show. Clowns entertained us between the acts of bareback riders on horses, lions in a cage with their tamer, beautiful elephants, trapeze artists and a man and woman walking a tight rope, high up, in the top of the tent.

Half way through he show there was an interval when Alfie mentioned to me that he needed to go to the toilet. I stood up to take him but he announced that now he was eight he was old enough to go by himself and no longer wished me to take him.

"Oh, I'm really not sure," I said, "I don't want you to get lost."

"I'll take him," offered John.

Whilst the boys went to look for the toilet Ada said, "Hells Bells, I wouldn't fancy swinging on that trapeze. One hell of a height. Kill you if you fell."

"Me neither," I agreed, "I've never been one for heights."

Ada then said, "Mind you a trapeze wouldn't 'arf spice up your sex life – but not so high up. Just imagine it, swinging in for a shag."

"I think you're letting your imagination run away with you," I said laughing. "Shush now here are the boys."

The boys returned to the plank seats looking sheepish and giggling.

"What have you two been up to?" I asked them.

"Us? Nothing," they replied together.

"Well something is going on. I can tell," I said.

"It wasn't us, it was the bloke," John said.

"A bloke, what bloke?" I said, starting to feel worried.

"A bloke in the toilets. He had his willy out, huge it was and he said to touch it," John explained.

"And did you?" I asked, horrified.

"No we did not," Alfie said, "Even though he said he'd give us a penny if we did."

Ada and I exchanged a concerned look and she mouthed to me, "Dirty bugger," I nodded in response.

Concentrating on the second half of the circus performance became difficult as I hated any thought of the boys being in danger.

The grand finale was spectacular; all the performers filled the circus ring and we applauded, following which Ada said, "Come on, who's up for an ice cream, my treat?"

We enjoyed ice creams topped with sarsaparilla sauce, or 'monkey's blood' the boys called it, as the four of us wandered around the fairground. Our attention was caught by a circle of onlookers watching two people fighting. The crowd was cheering them on and shouting advice such as, "Give 'im one, smash 'is face in, go on give 'im a good punchin".

As we drew closer I noticed one of the fighters was a woman and as she punched her opponent under his jaw with a thwack from a left hook, down he went.

The delighted crowd cheered even louder, stamped their feet and applauded the victor.

John and Alfie, jumping up and down, shouted, "That's him, that's the man."

The sound of a police whistle bringing Bryn Davis to the scene caused the crowd to slowly disperse. Police officer Davis helped the dazed man to his feet and enquired what the fight was all about.

"She attacked me for no reason at all," said the man whose lip was beginning to swell and whose nose was now bleeding.

"No reason, no reason you dirty bugger!" the woman shouted. "Exposing himself he was officer, to little lads. There's them here who'll bear witness. So don't believe him."

The man hung his head. Bryn began to take his notebook from his pocket and was then momentarily interrupted by a passer-by who confirmed the fact that the flasher had been exposing himself in the toilets.

Quick as lightning, and before she could be stopped, the woman grabbed the man by his tie and roughly pinned him up against the wall of a side show, then screamed into his face, "Show your face or your dick 'round here again and I'll chop the bugger off and ram it down your throat."

"Now, now," said Bryn taking charge, "I think, young man, you and I will go over to the police station for a chat. As for you madam, please try to keep the peace."

I recognised the woman as she walked towards us and knew that there was no doubt she would indeed keep her threat to the 'flasher'.

"Hello Betty," she said, brushing down her skirt.

"Come and meet your grandmother boys," I said to John and Alfie who hadn't seen Lucrettia Flitch since they were ill with whooping cough over two years before.

Lucrettia and Horace Flitch were now the owners of a boxing booth. Horace sat in a cabin selling tickets whilst Lucrettia walked up and down handing out leaflets and shouting, *"roll up, roll up, go a round – win a pound."*

Terrance, their prize fighter, dressed in shorts, vest and boxing pumps paraded up and down the stage, flexing his muscles and looking menacing.

Flushed with pride at her success at apprehending the flasher Lucrettia Flitch seemed to be in a more mellow mood than I had ever witnessed before.

"Fancy meeting you here, Betty Dawson," she said. (I hated being called Betty and she knew it.)

"We've just been to the circus. I didn't know you were running a boxing booth," I said.

"Oh yes. Got to do something to keep the wolf from the door," she replied, then shouted to those around the booth, "roll up, roll up, go a round win a pound."

Ada asked, "How did you learn about boxing Mrs Flitch? You've got a mean left hook."

"It was my dear old dad. He ran a boxing booth, this very booth in fact. It's been in storage but just look at the queue, very popular boxing is, very popular," she replied.

"Does anyone ever win a pound?" John asked.

"Very rarely," Mrs Flitch said, "except in the collieries, those miners have arms like pit props, solid muscle they are. What's more they take their boxing very serious they do. The Durham Miners Gala I think it was, one won a pound and bought a wedding ring for his lass."

"Now that's romantic," commented Ada.

"Where do you live?" Alfie asked.

"Oh we have a beautiful caravan, beautiful it is. Come on lads I'll show you," Lucrettia Flitch said.

Although we had not been included in the invitation to view the 'beautiful caravan' Ada and I followed the boys.

I noticed, as we passed the stage, that Terrance was now skipping fast between showing a few boxing moves; we walked around the boxing booth to the caravan which was located behind the boxing ring.'

Lucrettia and Horace's home was well appointed if rather overfull with ornaments, mostly made of crystal.

The boys were offered juice which they accepted. Ada and I were offered tea which we declined. Mrs Flitch was presenting her more charming side which I had never witnessed before and it aroused my suspicions.

"So what's been happening in your life since I last saw you Betty?" she asked.

"Nothing much," I replied, having already decided to tell her nothing and slipping my left hand into my pocket.

"Well you are engaged to Adam," Alfie said.

"En…gaaaag…ed!" Flitch said, dragging the word out.

"And John goes to the grammar school," Alfie added.

"Grammaaaaar shool," she said, smiling sweetly at John.

"What a clever boy, just like his father," she went on. "Who, by the way, is still on holiday in Durham, at 'His Majesty's Pleasure' thanks to you Betty Dawson," she directed at me with a snarl.

I knew the conviviality wouldn't last, she had resumed her natural dislike of me, so we said our goodbyes.

Her parting remark to the boys was, "I'm always looking for strong lads to help with the boxing booth. So think on boys, the pay is good."

I felt me knees go weak at the thought of the boys living and working on the fairground and needed to hold onto Ada's arm for support.

Later when we were back at Providence House we told Agatha about our encounter with Lucrettia Flitch.

"I didn't think she would ever show her face in this area again," Agatha said.

Ada and I agreed. A conversation and discussion followed about installing a telephone for Agatha, now that she was living alone.

"It would give me peace of mind," I said, in what I hoped was a persuasive tone.

"I know you worry," said Agatha, "I suppose you're right and the good thing would be that Frank could contact me if she needed to."

"Any word of Frank?" Ada asked.

"Not really," replied Agatha, "other than I heard her doctor friend picks her up from the pharmacy sometimes and that he is very good looking, Maureen who works in the chemist shop told me; and he has an unusual name."

"How unusual?" I asked.

"Posslethwaite I think, or something like it," Agatha said,

adding, "maybe Smurthwaite or Haverthwaite, can't really remember except it ended in thwaite."

"Could it have been Thistlethwaite?" I asked.

"Yes, that's it," she replied. "Apparently he's met Frank's parents and, according to Maureen, they really like him."

Ada and I decided to investigate Dr Thistlethwaite further, or the Dr Thistlethwaite who might be his brother or cousin, but not to mention it to Agatha at this stage.

8
Esther

The end of October 1935; Bonny had almost completed her operating theatre training at the Morgan Endowment Hospital and had enjoyed living at home and being back in Ransington. Sometimes we would go to the pictures and always enjoyed musicals such as 'Old Man Rhythm' or 'Stars Over Broadway'.

The Pathe news told of Mussolini invading Ethiopia and the rise of the Hitler Youth in Germany. Disappointingly there was no news of the Prince of Wales and his new mistress. The news from America, which Delicia's mother regularly sent her by letter, was that the affair between the Prince and Mrs Simpson was serious even though she was married.

One Monday morning, whilst helping Mrs Scribbins with the washing she said, "Do you think you could do me a favour Miss Bettina, well it's more a favour of your friend Bonny. The friend who used to work here but she's a nurse now?"

"Ask away," I said, turning the heavy mangle whilst she fed the clothes through.

"Well it's me friend and neighbour Esther. She's got a problem but won't see a doctor."

"What kind of problem?" I asked.

"Well hit's personal like. You know down below," she whispered. "Won't go to a doctor, can't hafford it I suppose.

'er man and 'er lads works down t docks; only gets a shift if t gaffer is takin on."

"Bonny is still in training so I don't quite know what she could do," I said.

"She might be able to talk 'er into seein' a doctor. I'll lend Esther the money," Mrs Scribbins said.

"I'll ask Bonny, but can't make any promises, if she can go it will be in the morning," I said to a clearly concerned Mrs Scribbins.

The following day Bonny was on a 'late' which meant she started work at 1pm.

At 10am we drove into Mrs Scribbins street and stopped the car outside her flat.

Mrs Scribbins was sitting on a stool on the freshly swilled pavement waiting for us to arrive.

Smiling she said, "Just go in, Esther is expecting you. I'm going in late to Iona 'ouse to hiron, all arranged with Lady McLeod. I'll just sit 'ere and keep an eye on the car for you."

The street looked decrepit and dirty with litter everywhere. However I noticed that both Mrs Scribbins and her neighbour Esther's steps had been recently scrubbed and edged with donkey stone.

We knocked on Esther's door and went in. She was in bed, looking poorly, and I introduced myself and Bonny to her. I explained that Bonny was training to be a nurse and, as friends of Mrs Scribbins, we hoped we could help.

Bonny asked, "What exactly seems to be problem Esther?"

"Well it's down below, I've had it for years. Used to be able to push it back inside but it's too big now. I had a haemorrhage over the weekend," Esther explained.

"Didn't you tell your family?" asked Bonny.

"No there's only me 'usband and me two lads. Men don't want to be troubled with women's problems," she replied.

Bonny had recently completed several weeks working on the gynaecological ward at the Royal Victoria Infirmary, where she was training, and told Esther this to reassure her.

Esther then showed us the problem, which was a prolapsed uterus the size of a football. I was both amazed and impressed at how calm Bonny looked.

As for me, I felt anything but calm, never having seen anything like it before.

"Your womb has prolapsed and you need to be in hospital," Bonny said in a kind but matter of fact tone.

"No, not the Ransington Infirmary, I'm not going there. You come out feet first, I'm not going there," Esther kept saying, obviously afraid.

"Well, shall I arrange for Dr Salmon to visit you here at home?" Bonny said.

"No. Can't you push it back in for me nurse. I've put a bowl of water, soap and a towel on the side for you," Esther pleaded. "I need to get back to my cleaning job at Judge Mcleods."

"Oh yes," I said, "I remember Mrs Scribbins said you were working up at Hampton House."

"I've sent a message to say I'm not well but will be back soon. Can't you at least just push it back for me nurse?" Esther pleaded with Bonny.

"I'm afraid your prolapse is ulcerated and there is some infection which needs to be attended to first," Bonny said kindly.

"What will I do then? I need my wages coming in." Esther was becoming quite upset.

Three loud knocks on the front door broke the impasse.

Opening the door I found a barefoot waif of a girl standing there. She was dressed in rags; but under her mass of matted, filthy hair a pretty face with bright green eyes shone through the grime. I estimated her age to be about 11 years old.

"Can I help you?" I asked.

"Me ma says can Esther lend er a slice o' bread," the child said.

"Wait here, I'll go and ask her," I replied. "Who shall I say it is?"

"Me name's Em," she replied, wiping her nose on the sleeve of her dirty, tattered cardigan.

I explained to Esther and she said, "There's a loaf in the kitchen cupboard. Give her a slice off that."

There was very little food in the cupboard other than the loaf of bread which I cut a slice from and gave it to the girl.

Esther said, "Poor as church mice that lot are and another baby on the way. Live off the welfare mostly."

Bonny took charge saying, "Now Esther I'm going to ask Dr Moshe Salmon to call and see you later to-day. Have a chat with him and see what you think.

"Thank you nurse and thank you Miss Dawson," Esther said as we left.

Mrs Scribbins was still sitting on the stool by her step watching my car and we told her that the doctor would be calling to see Esther later in the day.

Bonny went to the telephone box and, after explaining the problem, asked Moshe to call on Esther as a matter of urgency. She then travelled, by tram, to her work in the operating theatre of the Morgan Endowment hospital.

I went straight to see Ian in his chambers and luckily he was in and able to see me. I told him that Esther needed to be in hospital but that she had a fear of the Ransington Infirmary.

"I hope you feel you can help, Ian, as she can't even afford to pay for the doctor. However Bonny is arranging for Moshe to call on Esther today," I said.

"Poor Esther, I didn't realise she was so ill. I rarely see her as she cleans the house whilst I'm at work and has done so for years. She has a key and is most trustworthy, keeps the place immaculate, I just leave her money on the kitchen table," Ian said.

"She really needs to see Mr Sturgis at the Morgan," I said, feeling bold. "The sooner she is better the sooner she will be back looking after Hampton House."

Ian looked thoughtful for a moment then said, "Leave it to me Bettina, I'll phone Moshe and ask him to arrange for Esther to be admitted to the Morgan under the care of Mr Sturgis and I will foot the bill."

"Thank you, thank you Ian," I said, "I'll go and let Esther know."

Esther looked shocked when I told her that Ian was arranging for her to be admitted to the Morgan.

"But I avn't got a nightie and it'll be posh there," she exclaimed with panic in her voice.

I then noticed she was wearing an old cotton frock.

"Bought it at a jumble sale," Esther explained, then said, "I'll need to let me 'usband know."

"Where does he work? I'll go and tell him," I said

"No he won't be working, there's none been taken on today. 'Im and the lads 'll be in the 'ope and Anchor down the street," she said, "Little Em, two doors down, she'll run a message, I'll go and ask her."

"No I'll go," I said, "you just stay in bed."

I knocked on a filthy front door, two down from Esther and little Em answered.

"Esther has to go into hospital, please will you go and tell her husband in the Hope and Anchor?" I asked Em.

"Who is it?" a woman's voice shouted from inside the house.

"Esther 'as to go into the 'ospital and this lady wants me to go and tell 'er 'usband," Em shouted back.

A pregnant woman came to the door smoking a cigarette.

"It'll cost you a tanner," she said, looking me up and down.

I handed Em a sixpence and as she ran, bare foot, towards the Hope and Anchor the woman shouted after her, "Em, mind and get me five Woodbines whilst you're there."

I then returned to Iona House where Mrs Scribbins had almost finishing the ironing and I gave her the news.

"I'm that pleased Miss Bettina. That 'usband of 'ers is useless and so are 'er lads. Think more of their ale than a days work," Mrs Scribbins said.

"Please would you iron those two nightdresses of mine whilst I go and pack a bag with toiletries, slippers and dressing gown, Mrs Scribbins, we can't have Esther going into hospital without her essentials now can we," I said, then dashed upstairs.

Mrs Scribbins and I went back to Esther's flat and, together, we helped her into my little Morris car.

Moshe had called and a bed was waiting for Esther on the female ward at the Morgan where she would be in the care of Mr Sturgis, the renowned gynaecologist and obstetrician.

The huge prolapse was swabbed and dressed several times daily with acraflavene. It reduced in size and after one week Esther had her operation; a hysterectomy, from which she recovered well.

Ian visited with fruit and flowers, as did I.

Mrs Scribbins visited her friend and neighbour every evening and stayed for the full visiting time. So impressed was she with the care Esther received that she made enquiries about becoming an evening volunteer at the hospital.

Esther's husband visited her once during her stay in hospital; her sons not at all. Their fear of hospitals, combined with their love of The Hope and Anchor kept them away.

9

Logan

November 1935 and there was a knock on the kitchen door of Iona House. I answered it to a young boy who had a Scottish Terrier on a lead; he handed me an envelope. The contents read:-

Dear Miss Dawson,

Matron has had a severe stroke and is in hospital. I recall how well Logan got on with your dog Pip so please can you take him. If you can't he will have to go to the shelter for dogs as we can't keep him here at Alpine Lodge.

Yours sincerely,

N. Cotton
Acting Matron.

I thanked the boy then took Logan into the house.

The same day a letter arrived for me from Adam:-

Circlet of Gold

3 Shiney Row,
Denstag.
November 7th, 1935.

My Darling Bettina,

I'm sorry our weekend in Northumberland turned out the way it did.

It was totally my fault as I had no idea you would not want to live in America.

I was aware that you feel responsible for John and Alfie, although I had not realised just how much.

That is the trouble with not seeing each other for such a long time.

I shall be staying here in Denstag for a few more days as father is ill with bronchitis then I have to go to London to meet with Nick Van der Linden. He is opening a branch of his business here in England, the investment side of things, and I have expressed an interest. I spoke to Nick on the telephone and have told him I won't be accepting the job in Chicago.

However I do need to return to America to complete my studies at Harvard and tie up some ends of work I've been doing for Nick.

I love you and want us to have a wedding we will remember for ever as being the happiest day of our lives.

Your business plan with Agatha sounds interesting and I wish you every success with it. Perhaps you could tell me more in your letters to me.

I sail for America in a weeks time so will miss your birthday and for that I'm sorry.

Always remember I love you from the bottom of my heart.

Love, Adam xxxx

Agatha, using her newly installed telephone, excitedly informed me that the bales of silk cloth had arrived from Macclesfield; with the exception of one bale which was to follow. Also there had been an enquiry from a Lady Dillmont-Preast who had been a friend of Lady Rachael, and would like an appointment for her twin daughters.

"The twins will be 'coming out' as débutantes and Lady Dillmont-Preast is interested in our silk underwear for them," Agatha said excitedly.

The following morning, with Pip and Logan beside me, my sewing machine and Agatha's lace safely stored on the back seat, I motored to Little Laxlet. We would discuss the running of our business, which Agatha and I had decided to call 'Lingerie Chic'.

The bales of silk, now in the sewing room at Providence House, were extravagantly lustrous and totally beautiful. Following careful inspection we decided to cover and protect them with a sheet.

I explained to Agatha why Logan was with me and she said she wouldn't mind if he stayed with her for company. Now she was living on her own she felt lonely at times. I agreed it would be a good idea if she wanted him to, but to say if it wasn't working out then we would think of something else for the dog.

Providence House looked wonderful since its renovation and Agatha was managing to cook with the Aga, even admitting that she was enjoying using it. The kitchen smelled of freshly baked, spicy ginger biscuits and an egg and bacon pie was cooling on the side ready for our lunch.

"Have you heard, Ada's going out with Emrys Davis?" Agatha said.

"Yes, Ada told me in a letter, although I haven't seen her in a while," I replied.

"They make a lovely couple, Emrys and Ada. I hope it works out for them better than it did with Albert Dixon," Agatha said.

"Mmm," I responded, munching on a ginger biscuit.

"No idea what went wrong there, he seemed so keen on her," Agatha continued.

"Any news of Frank?" I asked, over our cuppa.

"Only bits and pieces I hear when I'm in Burside, I miss Frank and the car," she said with a sad sigh, adding, "I said she might as well keep it as I can't drive so it's no use to me. Shame as we'd had the stable and apple store converted into a garage."

"Never mind," I said. "I'll leave my car in the garage when I'm here in the winter." Then asking, "Do you think she's still going out with the doctor?"

"As far as I know she is. Hilda was in the chemist shop the other day and she says Frank is now wearing a ring on her engagement finger," Agatha said.

"That's been quick," I said, whilst thinking, 'It can't be the same Dr Thistlethwaite, he must have a brother or a cousin'.

Advertising and marketing were on the agenda for discussion at our business meeting. A decision was made to place an advertisement in 'The Lady' magazine and I would ask 'Fiskers', the exclusive dress shop in Ransington, if they would consider placing a few business cards on their coffee table beside the gold painted sofas.

The sound of a motorbike stopping outside interrupted our meeting, followed by three loud bangs on the front door. I opened it to the rider of the motor bike which I noticed had a side-car. Under the leather hat, goggles, flying jacket, trousers and knee high boots was Charlie Hadleigh from Macclesfield, standing on the doorstep carrying a bale of silk and an overnight bag.

"Come in, it's good to see you," I said.

"Will you stay for a bite to eat ?" Agatha asked.

"Aye, I will that, and overnight as well if you'll have me. I've taken a couple of days off that's due to me and I don't know this part of the world at all," replied Charlie.

Agatha seemed delighted with Charlie's disconcertingly direct approach and I detected a hint of attraction between them as Agatha was coquettishly inclining her head and patting her hair.

Charlie said, "I broke my journey in Harrogate and had lunch in Betty's Tea Rooms. I'd heard about Betty's and very good it was too. I've brought a couple of Yorkshire curd cakes, thought they'd do nicely for us tea." She then placed two large Yorkshire curd cakes on the kitchen table.

"I'll just take Pip and Logan out to stretch their legs for a while, is that okay with you?" I asked, " then we can continue with our meeting when I get back."

The village of Little Laxlet never failed to charm me. Now in its winter colours we scuffed through the fallen leaves. Pip sniffed every gate post and corner, as she always did, enjoying her walk; Logan doing much the same. The smell of poplars, closing down for the winter, wafted across from those lining the boundary of Cuthbert's field. A memory of taking the boys there to play on instruction from Mrs Flitch the day of my mother's funeral came flooding back to me. It was when she gave my baby sister away but, as it happened, that turned out lucky for us.

The old chestnut tree by the chapel had dropped hundreds of conkers; ideal for John and Alfie I thought whilst gathering some into a crocheted bag I always carried in my pocket.

Standing on the village green with Pip and Logan I looked across at the stone houses and cottages, wisps of smoke exiting the chimneys, shrubs and trees almost naked, the smell of a bonfire. The mantle of winter, yet still beautiful.

I knocked on the door of Hilda's cottage and she took a little while to answer, wearing a towel over her head when she did.

"Oh Bettina, don't come in, I'm full of germs. Only a cold but I feel rough. I was having a Vick inhalation," she said, sounding very blocked in her nose.

"Sorry about your cold," I said, "is there anything I can get you?"

"No thank you. I'll be fine before long."

"We're having a business meeting over at Providence House. The lady from the silk factory is there too," I said.

"A business meeting, now that sounds important. How's Agatha.? Did you know Frank's engaged? Did you know Ada and Emrys are courting?" Hilda said whilst gasping for breath and sneezing.

"Agatha is okay thanks Hilda. I had heard Frank was engaged and you've confirmed it. Good news about Ada and Emrys," I said.

"It is that," Hilda said. "I never thought Albert Dixon was right for her. There's a new tenant next door at Groat Cottage, a man, works at the airfield. On his own, family to follow."

Hilda then broke into a fit of coughing.

"Oh Hilda please go in. We'll catch up properly when

you're better. I'll be in Little Laxlet more, now that we've started the business."

Agatha and Charlie had set out the sewing room with three chairs around the table, a notepad, pencil and agenda for each of us.

The meeting went well.

Publicity – Advertisement in 'The Lady'. Business cards in dress shops and milliners in Ransington, Harrogate and York.

Pricing – make a comparative study of our competitors then decide.

Accounts – As I was familiar with keeping accounts that would be my job. An accounts ledger to be purchased.

Patterns – Charlie suggested wooden templates. When output increased paper patterns would be impractical. She knew someone who would make them.

We then looked at the paper patterns for tap pants, nightdresses and cami-knickers I had brought. We chose a selection and handed them to Charlie to be copied in wood.

Packaging – Pretty and feminine. Pink tissue paper, lavender and/or hearts. Final wrapping to be brown paper and string.

The meeting concluded and I said, "I must leave you now and go back to Ransington to see John and Alfie."

"In that case," Charlie said, running her fingers through her shining, cropped, dark hair, "how about we go over to the pub tonight for a drink, we can take Logan?"

A look of panic immediately shot across Agatha's face; silence was her immediate response.

She then said, "I've never been in a pub before."

"Never been in a pub before!" exclaimed Charlie. "Well it's time you did. We can go further afield if you like but that 'Shoulder of Mutton' over there looks alright. Do they have a snug?"

"I've no idea," said Agatha.

"Then there's only one way to find out. Personally I like a pint myself but you have whatever you fancy," Charlie said. "We can talk over all the trips we're going on."

"Trips. What trips?" asked a bemused Agatha.

"Trips taking out business cards for 'Lingerie Chic'. We'll go to Harrogate and York, find some posh dress and hat shops. We can have tea in Betty's Tea rooms," said Charlie.

As I drove out of Little Laxlet; Pip alongside me, I had a feeling that Agatha was about to embark on a new phase in her life, with Charlie a friend and perhaps companion. Logan had made himself at home and when I left he was asleep and comfortable on a blanket in the corner of the kitchen having enjoyed a bowl of freshly cooked beef mince.

Then my thoughts drifted to Adam and how our life now seemed so complicated.

However, not only had I a need to focus on driving in the dark with care, but I also had an important telephone call to make that evening; to our first prospective customer, Lady Dillmont-Preast.

10

The Donkey

November 15th, 1935 and the day before my birthday. To celebrate, my friend Ada was calling and we planned to spend the day together. Several birthday cards had already arrived, some of which contained letters; I recognised one as being from my friend Delicia.

Rock Castle,
Scotland.
November 10th, 1935.

My Dear Bettina,

Just to wish you a Happy Birthday, hope you like the card and photograph.

Jude brings us such joy and at 1yr and 1month has just taken his first steps which I consider to be very advanced.

We will be visiting aunt Eliza Jane for Christmas and it would be wonderful to see you and the boys.

Hope all is going well with you and Adam. Dad visited us here recently but refused to be drawn into any discussion regarding Adam and his future. However I did have the distinct feeling that dad considers him to be an impressive young man. (Those were his exact words)

Have a wonderful birthday.

Love, Delicia. xxxx

The photograph of Jude made my heart turn over and I would be sticking it in the photograph album with all the others Delicia had sent me over the past year.

The business cards for 'Lingerie Chic' had arrived by post that morning and I was very pleased with the printing and the message which the cards conveyed.

Whilst waiting for Ada to arrive I made a list of places where I hoped to distribute the business cards including, 'Fiskers' the designer dress shop, 'Trebbles' an exclusive milliners and 'Maurice' the most fashionable hair stylist in town.

*

Ada arrived, rosy cheeked, smiling and wearing a smart day dress in shades of green. Her dark brown hair cascaded in soft curls around her shoulders and she smelt wonderful.

"It's Vol de Nuit," Ada told me. "Vol de Nuit and very expensive, Emrys bought it for me."

'Ada's romance with Emrys must be going well.' I thought.

"Happy Birthday for tomorrow," Ada said, putting a huge, heavy parcel in front of me.

"Shall I save it or open it?" I asked.

"Open it, open it!" was her excited reply.

"How on earth did you manage to carry this all the way on the train?" I asked, whilst opening the heavy parcel.

"Ah well, I didn't exactly come on the train. Emrys brought me in a police car," she explained.

"Is that even allowed?" I asked.

"Not really, but one was going in for service so I hitched a lift," she said.

The gift was a floor-standing, angle poise lamp.

"I knew you'd need a good light for your sewing with the underwear business so it's a bit of a practical present I realise that. Here I got you this as well, sorry I didn't have time to wrap it up," she said, handing me a jar of Yardley's lavender bath salts.

The various shops we took the 'Lingerie Chic' business cards to all agreed to display them and even hand them out. We then called at the restaurant in the department store for lunch and to catch up with each others news.

"Adam was meant to be coming here tomorrow and we were supposed to be going to a dinner dance at the Metropole Hotel," I said.

"What do you mean, 'supposed to be' isn't he coming now?" was Ada's surprised response.

"No he had to go to London then back to America to finish his studies at Harvard. "I answered.

"Well that's a bit of a bugger. Do you think he's taken the huff 'cause you won't go and live in America?" she asked.

"Not sure," I replied, "he's certainly disappointed about it, that I do know; but there might be a chance of a job here in England with Nick Van der Linden," I said.

"That sounds more like it but I hope it's not in bloody London, I'd never see you."Ada said.

To change the subject I said, "Delicia is visiting aunt Eliza Jane's for Christmas."

"Oh lovely, I must try to get to see her. How old is the baby now?" Ada asked.

"One year and one month," I answered, showing her the photograph of Jude.

"He's gorgeous," Ada said, "I'll have to get cracking if I'm going to have a baby before I'm twenty one."

"You'll be twenty in June next year so you still have time. Anyway how is it going with Emrys?" I asked.

"All right, except he's a bit shy," she answered.

"Shy, how shy?" I asked.

"Very shy. Says he respects women, all women but especially me," she said, rolling her eyes.

"Well that's good isn't it?" I said, feeling that it probably wasn't as good as I'd hoped.

"I suppose so but I would like him to put in a bit more effort into our love life. You know, the intimate side of things," Ada said.

"Meaning?" I asked, wondering how explicit Ada proposed to be.

"He does work funny hours and I respect the fact that when we are at work we have to act professional like. I can understand that," she said.

I could feel a 'but' coming on.

"But," Ada said, "I'd like him to take me in his arms, sweep me off me feet; you know like they do at the pictures."

"Perhaps Emrys is not 'the one' then, or do you want to give the romance a bit more time to blossom?" I suggested in what I hoped was an understanding manner.

"Not sure," she said, then asked, "Do you think I'm being impatient?"

"Only you know that. Aunt Eliza Jane says true love doesn't always run smoothly. Only time will tell," I said.

"I know, but how much fucking time does he need," she retorted.

I could detect her patience was running low!

We decided to walk back to Iona House.

Living in the country was quiet for Ada and she enjoyed

the opportunity to browse in the large variety of shops we had in Ransington.

A braying donkey interrupted our leisurely walk as we window-shopped in the High Street.

As we approached it the distress of the poor animal was very apparent. A man was beating the donkey with a long stick and shouting at it in a cruel manner.

The poor donkey carried a heavy load on its back, at least double that of what the small animal should be carrying.

"Gan on, gan on, you stupid bugger," shouted the man, whilst whacking the donkey on its hind quarters.

The little donkey just stood there, too exhausted to move.

Quick as a flash Ada darted from the pavement into the road and grabbed the man's arm, preventing him from hitting the donkey.

"What the hell do you think you're doing?" she shouted at the man. "How would you like it if I hit you with a stick?"

"Stupid animal," said the man, "anyway, what's it got to do with you, you interfering cow?"

"That load is too heavy for him, he's shattered, he's too thin and you are fucking cruel," Ada retorted.

"It's nowt to do with you," the man insisted.

"Nowt to do with me, I'll tell you what its got to do with me. You are abusing that donkey, his ribs are sticking out and his feet need trimming," shouted Ada, grabbing the stick from the man and snapping it over her thigh.

"I repeat," said the man, "nowt to do with you."

They both stood their ground.

"Now I suggest you listen to me and listen good," Ada said to the man, in a calmer voice, adding "My boyfriend is a copper and you are a cruel bastard. This donkey needs retiring to a quiet meadow. So what are you going to do?"

"What am I going to do? I'll show you what I'm going to do, you interfering bitch of a woman," he said, removing the panniers from the donkey's back.

"What am I going to do," the man continued, "what I'm going to do is to give 'im away. You can 'ave 'im."

The man walked away leaving the panniers on the pavement.

The little donkey made no attempt to follow him.

"Looks like you've got yourself a donkey," I said, looking at the pathetic creature standing beside us.

"Well bugger me, I never thought that would happen," said Ada, taking hold of the bridle.

Slowly we led the donkey back to Iona House.

Vera, Mabel and Ivy, each carrying a triplet came into the garden to look at the donkey. Claudette and Rory followed with Mrs Handyside.

"Can we keep him, can we keep him?" squealed Claudette.

"I don't think so," said Vera, "he needs to be in a field."

Pip joined us in the garden and started to bark at the donkey until I picked her up.

The poor donkey was in such a state of exhaustion he did not even respond.

"I'm so sorry Vera," Ada said, "the man gave him to me so I'll have to sort it out."

Mr Handyside brought a bucket of water for the donkey and suggested the orchard might be a good place for him to graze.

We decided a cup of tea would help to 'sort it out' and around the kitchen table it was decided that we needed to get a message to Ada's dad who would bring the horse box and take the donkey, now named Eeyore by Claudette, back to the farm.

Ada made a telephone call to Burside police station. Mary on the switch board said she would pass on a message to Emrys who would be finishing his shift soon. She was sure Emrys would be perfectly happy to take a detour, cycle to Rookery Farm on his way home and ask Mr Smith to bring the horse box to Iona House.

We went into the orchard with an old horse blanket Mr Handyside had found in a shed. As Ada covered the donkey with the blanket she said, "Now don't you worry Eeyore. You'll be fine now. I'll look after you."

A sick animal really brought out the tender side of my friend; a tenderness I hoped she would find in her relationship with Emrys.

11

The Jardiniere

Lady Dillmont-Preast proved to be an excellent customer. Her twin daughters Arabella and Cordelia, aged 18yrs, required silk and lace underwear for their stay in Germany and Switzerland with an aristocratic family, the Petzlingers. The girls would be travelling to Switzerland in January 1936 for the skiing, followed by a year in Germany for the social season.

Agatha and I escorted the twins and their mother into the orangery of Providence House; their chauffeur, Baitman, waited in the Rolls Royce outside.

Lady Dillmont-Preast was dressed in furs with the distinct aroma of Shalimar and moth balls wafting from them. She seemed a formidable woman; by comparison the twins were quiet and shy.

I measured Arabella and Cordelia making notes of their measurements and requirements; white and pink being their mother's choice of colours for the underwear. Although I did notice Arabella looking longingly at the bale of red silk.

I attempted conversation, "Have you ever been skiing before?"

"Yes, several times. Count von Petzlinger has a lodge in the Swiss Alps," replied Lady Dillmont-Preast on behalf of her girls.

"Sounds wonderful," I said.

"Yes it is, as are the parties," said Arabella, who seemed less shy than her twin.

"The German men are so dashing, so well mannered," said Lady Dillmont-Preast.

"They sound charming," I said, wondering if these dashing, well mannered men were part of Fuhrer Hitler's Nazi party I'd heard so much about.

"Come now girls we need to make haste for our appointment for a dress fitting in Harrogate. Sadly lunch with Lady Rachael is not to be, so sad, so sad. We passed The Manor House on our way here, it looks quite forlorn," Lady Dillmont-Preast said, in a sombre tone.

Agatha and I each shook hands and thanked her Ladyship for her custom.

"Thank you so much Miss Dawson and Miss Dawson," she said, shaking our hands in her – now dressed in the finest cream kid gloved – hand. Adding, "a telephone call will suffice and Baitman will collect the garments next week."

"How the other half live," I said to Agatha over lunch.

"I know," she replied, "can you imagine it, all those parties."

"Sounds exhausting, but it's good for business. We've had several more enquiries, all friends of Lady Dillmont-Preast," I said.

"Logan has eaten three pounds," Agatha said.

"Three pounds of what?" I asked.

"£3 in money, three one pound notes. They were there on the window-sill, waiting to pay the butcher boy and Logan ate them," Agatha explained.

"Are you sure. How do you know it was him?" was my next question.

"He doesn't like the butcher boy so I try to keep the kitchen door shut to stop him running after the bike and snapping at the boy's ankles," she said.

"Good idea, but how do you know he ate the pound notes?"

"The butcher boy knocked on the kitchen door, Logan went berserk as usual, running up and down the windowsill barking his head off and I thought the money had fallen on the floor. Couldn't find it but luckily I had more in my purse. When we went for our walk Logan 'pooped' and there was the evidence, chewed up, undigested pound notes." Agatha said.

"Oh dear. He's a bit of a liability," I said, adding, "Are you sure you want to keep him?"

"I do but I'll certainly keep money out of his way now," she said.

"I agree, he makes a lousy money box," I said, pleased Agatha could see the funny side.

"What are you doing for Christmas?" Agatha asked.

"I'll be at Iona House I expect. Although I'm hoping to visit aunt Eliza Jane in Gosforth, as Delicia and Ralph will be there with Jude. What about you?" I enquired.

"Either Charlie will be coming to stay here or Logan and I have been invited to spend Christmas with her family in Macclesfield," she replied.

"That sounds lovely," I said, "but keep him away from the Christmas presents."

"Have you heard about Frank's engagement?" Agatha asked.

"Sadly, I have. It seems as though the pressure from her parents is working," I answered.

"Charlie is a great comfort to me, she understands how it is to love another woman. We don't think Frank will settle into marriage, in fact we think she'll hate it," Agatha said.

"Only time will tell," I said, thinking 'I seem to have been saying that a lot lately'.

"Have you met the new tenants at Groat Cottage yet?" I asked Agatha.

"Yes, and a scruffy bunch they are too. The wife looks as though she's expecting and she had a black eye the last time I saw her," Agatha replied.

"That sounds awful," I said.

"There's a little girl there as well and they're always on the scrounge from Hilda; you know what a soft touch she is, I'm sure she must be out of pocket," said Agatha.

"Where did they come from?" I asked.

"Moved here from Ransington. Husband works at the new airfield," answered Agatha.

"Poor Hilda, I'll call on her when I walk Pip and Logan this afternoon," I said.

Hilda greeted Pip, Logan and me warmly, invited us in and insisted on making a cup of tea. She was now over her cold but I sensed something was bothering her.

"It's the new neighbours next door," she said before I'd even enquired about them.

The borrowing was becoming a problem so I just listened.

"She sends the child, Em, who as far as I can tell doesn't go to school. The husband is as rough as 'a badgers bum' if you'll pardon the expression and what's more he is violent."

'Poor Hilda,' I thought.

"Violent, has he ever been violent with you?" I asked.

"No, that's the funny thing. Nice as ninepence he is if we bump into each other. Nice as ninepence, even raises his hat. Seems to direct his anger at his wife," Hilda said.

"Well Hilda, I have to be going back to Ransington now but if ever you feel threatened by him please tell Jim at the pub and telephone me as well," I cautioned.

"I will," answered Hilda.

Arriving back at Iona House there was a letter waiting on the hall table and also a note with a message to telephone Ian.

The letter was from aunt Eliza Jane:-

High Stones,
Gosforth

December 3rd, 1935.

My Dear Bettina,

I am planning a Boxing Day party and wonder if you and the boys would like to join us. Winnie and Gladys are organising the games and of course there will be swimming. I have invited Vera and family and also Ian and his two boys.
Aaron and Jamila will be catering again to make things easier for me.
The evening will be given over to dancing. I have engaged a small band and Winnie, Gladys and their husbands are planning an exhibition dance. All very top secret although I've listened to the music and it seems to be in the Latin American genre.

Delicia and Ralph will be here with baby Jude so I hope you will come. We have plenty of room so you are welcome to stay for a few days if you wish.

Please could you send me the address of your friend Ada as Delicia has particularly asked me to include her on the guest list.

Your loving aunt,

Eliza Jane.

I telephoned Ian and was surprised at his request.

"Bettina it is over a year now since Dora passed away and, as yet, I haven't had the heart to sort out her clothes," he said.

"That's understandable," I said.

"Do you think you could do it for me, I would be ever so appreciative if you would?" he asked.

"Yes, of course I will," was my answer.

However knowing that Dora had had an extensive wardrobe I then asked Ian, "What would you like to do with Dora's things?"

"How do you mean?" he said.

"Well, would you like me to find a home for her things or sell them to raise money for charity?" I asked, feeling that I needed some sort of a clue from him.

"Haven't really thought about it but if you could go through everything and pack it all up then I'm happy for you to decide," Ian said.

The thought of being alone in Hampton House prompted my next question. "Would you mind if I take a friend with me for company?"

"Not at all, but I would like the job done before Seth and Edwin come home from school for their Christmas holiday," he answered.

"When will that be?" I asked.

"December 20th," was his reply.

"I could do it over a couple of weekends if that's okay with you," I said.

"Fine," he said, "I'll drop a key off for you at Iona House but I should be at home on Saturday. Don't worry though, I won't get in your way."

The following Saturday morning the electronic gates opened as if by magic as Ada and I drove, in my little Morris Minor, up the gravelled drive of Hampton House.

"Welcome girls," Ian said, showing us to Dora's dressing room; a room lined with wardrobes, full of the deceased Dora's clothes.

"I shall be going out shortly but help yourselves to food, there's plenty in the larder and fridge," he said.

On opening the first wardrobe the aroma of Chanel No. 5 drifted out; it was as though Dora had entered the room.

"Bloody creepy if you ask me," Ada said, packing garments into the boxes we had brought.

"I agree, it is, but at least we are helping Ian," I said.

"What charity did you say the money would be going to?" Ada asked.

"The orphanage, Alpine Lodge Orphanage. Dora was a governor there. Her friends in the Ladies League of Health and Beauty have agreed to hold an auction," I said.

We kept removing hanger after hanger of hardly worn clothes.

"That oil painting on the landing is a bit unnerving. It's as if Dora is watching us," said Ada.

"It is a bit, but I'm sure you'll agree she was a beautiful woman," I said.

"Personally I thought she was full of herself and up her own arse, full of her own importance. If you know what I mean," Ada said, as we continued to pack the clothes.

"I can't disagree with you," I said, not having been Dora's greatest fan, "but Ian loved her. Vera once told me that 'Love is Blind' and Ian's love for Dora certainly was blind."

As we continued packing it became apparent that more boxes would be required.

"I wonder if Ian would mind if Mabel and Ivy had some of these things," I said.

"I'm sure he wouldn't. Perhaps Mrs Scribbins and Esther could choose something as well," added Ada.

"That's a good idea. Mrs Scribbins is starting voluntary work at the Morgan soon and I'm sure she would welcome a smart outfit," I said.

"What kind of voluntary work?" Ada asked.

"She hasn't really said but I think the volunteers push a trolley around the wards at visiting time to sell magazines and sweets to the patients and their visitors," I said.

"What makes her want to do that?" Ada asked.

"She was so impressed with the care her friend Esther received when she was a patient there, Mrs Scribbins just wants to help," I answered.

"Well I've heard the volunteers at the Morgan are all a bit la-di-da so I hope she'll fit in okay," Ada said, walking into the bedroom and opening the drawers of the tall-boy.

"Does Ian want us to sort out the undies as well?" Ada asked. "Just look at these nightdresses, they're fab. All silk and ... *OH!* just come and look in this drawer – it's full of French knickers. Oo la la – looks like black was her favourite – or maybe his!"

"Not sure, I'll phone him later," I replied.

We packed the full boxes into the car ready to take to Alpine Lodge with a few outfits put to one side for Mabel, Ivy, Mrs Scribbins and Esther to look at.

"Fell on her feet did Dora," said Ada, as we sat in the drawing room with a sandwich made from some cold salmon we found in the fridge.

"I know, it's a lovely house," I said.

"Shame she had no fucking taste," Ada said.

"No taste," I said, feeling shocked, then adding, "Dora considered herself the epitome of good taste."

"Then tell me this then my friend," said Ada, pointing to the yellow and green Christopher Dresser jardinière and stand. "Why in hell's name did she buy a fucking piss pot on a stalk like that?"

A sentiment with which I had to agree and which made us laugh; quite what Dora would have thought of such a description of her valuable antique I couldn't imagine.

However, it was obvious Ada didn't care for it.

It took two full weekends to clear Dora's clothes. Ian always went out when we were there so we saw little of him other than a greeting when we first arrived.

A few days following the second weekend he expressed his appreciation with a card and a bouquet of flowers, hand delivered to Iona House for me and to Rookery Farm for Ada.

12

Boxing Day

A day with aunt Eliza Jane at High Stones in Gosforth was always something to look forward to.

With John, Alfie and Pip in the car we collected Ada from Rookery Farm on the way.

Our estimated time of arrival for the party was noon.

My one sadness being that Adam was in America and not sharing, what promised to be, an enjoyable family occasion with us.

"How are things?" I asked Ada.

"So, so," she replied.

"Only so, so," I said, wondering how this conversation might develop, bearing in mind the boys were in the back of the car.

"It's Emrys, we hardly see each other," Ada said, with sadness in her voice.

"I know the feeling," I replied.

"He's a bit of a disappointment. Well a *big* disappointment if you know what I mean."

"That's a shame," I said, whilst thinking, 'strange, she's been after him for ages.'

"Well I was hoping for a proposal at Christmas. Now that would have been so romantic. A Christmas engagement and a June wedding," Ada sighed.

"It didn't happen then?" I asked, already knowing the

answer. Then I added, "Now don't be glum. We are going to a party, staying the night and, guess what?"

"What?" asked Ada.

"Gladys and Winnie are performing an exhibition dance and I've heard on good authority that it could be Latin American," I said.

"You're kidding me. What with their twin husbands?" Ada exclaimed.

"Yes," I confirmed.

"Well, that'll be worth watching," Ada said, visibly cheering up.

There were several cars already in the drive when I parked my little Morris Minor. Delicia, Ralph and Jude arrived at the same time as us and we hugged and kissed, so happy to see each other again. Ralph held Jude in his arms and I knew the child had been adopted by the most perfect parents for him.

John and Alfie soon found Seth and Edwin and in no time all four boys were in the swimming pool.

The Boxing Day lunch was as fabulous as it was exotic. It consisted of a Yemeni buffet all cooked by Aaron and Jamila, who owned a nearby restaurant with Aaron's father Mohammed. The exquisite food made from recipes from their home country included lamb, chicken and fish dishes cooked in delicious spices, together with salads, flat breads and mouth watering desserts. The wonderful aromas and sight of the food was almost as good as the tastes and flavours.

Vera and Angus had brought Mabel and Ivy to help with the children, Claudette now 4 years, Rory aged 3 years and the triplets, Douglas, Caelan and Izzadora almost a year.

Claudette and Rory were both keen to swim and, each wearing a rubber ring, enjoyed splashing in the pool with Angus and Ian.

Following our amazing Boxing Day lunch aunt Eliza Jane said, "Bettina, would you be kind enough to accompany me around the garden? I need a short constitution and the path is slippery at this time of year."

We donned our coats and walked into the large garden where hellebores filled the borders and hung over the paths. Winter jasmine hugged the trellising against the walls of the house and a corkscrew witch hazel created a fabulous twisted form against the winter sky line. I was surprised at how much colour there was in December.

"Smell that," instructed aunt Eliza Jane, pointing to a leafless shrub which had small clusters of pink flowers hanging from the stems. The perfume was delectable and moving closer I noticed tiny blossoms, reminding me of aromatic pink pom -poms.

"Vibernum and I observe you are still wearing your engagement ring," said aunt Eliza Jane, then coming straight to the point, adding, "and how are things between you and Adam?"

"Hard to say. He's back in America and we do write to each other regularly," I replied.

"Mmm, I have a feeling in my old bones that all will be well between you two one of these days, and don't forget the family heirloom," she said.

"Family heirloom?" I queried.

"Yes, the Carrickmacross lace wedding veil. Your dear mother and grandmother both wore it on their wedding days," aunt said.

"So they did, and Delicia as well, didn't she make a stunning bride," I said, now remembering the veil Delicia had worn when she married Ralph.

We had now reached the farthest corner of the garden and rested on a bench next to a small woodland area. I could see that on the other side of the trees the grassy bank fell away steeply with a high hedge at the bottom. A further grassy bank arose up the other side; then beyond it the playing fields of the school.

"That's where King George and Queen Mary sleep," my aunt said, looking over to the steep grassy bank.

Immediately I felt concern due to having witnessed Lady Rachael begin her journey into dementia.

"Really," I said.

"Yes really. They do. It's a siding," she said.

"A siding. You mean a railway siding?" I asked.

"That is precisely what I mean. When the Royal train journeys to and from Scotland it stops here overnight," aunt explained, adding, "all top secret, very hush, hush."

This was beginning to be believable.

"We never see them of course, the train is well hidden, as you can see. But, yes my dear Bettina, this is where the King and Queen sleep, at the bottom of my garden," she said with a look of pure serenity on her face.

Aunt Eliza Jane seemed so pleased about the King and Queen's sleeping arrangements I could not help but feel happy for her.

As daylight faded and the evening celebrations were about to commence, Angus, Vera and their children left for home. The children, all tired, cuddled into Mabel and Ivy on the back seat of the Bentley.

"Lovely party," I said, rejoining Ada and Delicia then taking a sleepy Jude onto my lap.

"Certainly is," they both agreed.

"Any wedding date yet?" asked Delicia.

"Not yet. Adam will be home in the summer, so fingers crossed," I gave as my standard answer to a question I found myself being asked frequently.

"Dad said he had met Adam in London when he was opening a business there," Delicia said.

"Yes I knew he was meeting your dad. I think Adam is keen to work for him but in England," I said.

"Oh yes, I heard you had blocked any idea of living in America," Delicia said.

"I know, it's true and it does sound selfish but you see I am responsible for John and Alfie," I said.

"Tricky," said Delicia.

The band stopped playing quiet background music and the band leader announced that the exhibition dance would now be performed.

The band struck up with Brazilian Samba music. Winnie and Gladys, partnered by Cedric and Cyril, took to the floor. Both ladies were dressed in frilled ensembles, in shades of sunshine yellow and orange colours, short at the front and long at the back. On their heads each wore a large feathered headdress, again in shades of yellow and orange to match their dresses. The four exhibition dancers smiled at the audience and executed a perfect samba; changing partners from time to time just to confuse those of us watching.

I had changed, prior to the dancing, into a simple, dusky pink, silk flowered tea dress. With its V neck and cap sleeves this was my 'versatile dress' being adaptable for many different occasions.

Ada had brought, and was wearing, a full skirted, red spotted dress with flouncy net underskirts, and a wide black belt, accentuating her tiny waist. Her dark brown hair cascaded around her face and shoulders; she looked stunning.

I thought to myself, 'Why on earth doesn't Emrys propose? She's not going to hang around forever.'

I went to check on John and Alfie and they were playing chess with Seth and Edwin, as they said they would be.

Returning to the hall and the party I noticed that Ian was dancing the foxtrot with Ada. My friend loved dancing and observing them together I could see that Ian was a very competent dancer. 'Such a shame there is an age gap of twenty years,' I thought.

Over the course of the evening Ian also danced with me and several other guests, but he always returned to Ada.

We stayed overnight at High Stones, Ada and me sharing a twin bedroom.

Once in the privacy of our beds I said, "It was good to see Ian enjoying himself tonight."

"He's a lovely dancer," Ada said, "such a firm hold."

"Shame he's so much older than you," I said.

"Many a good tune played on an old fiddle," Ada answered.

"Ada Smith. Do you mean what I think you mean?" was my surprised response.

"Could do," she sleepily said.

"But what about Emrys?" I asked.

"Emrys who?" she answered, then fell asleep.

13

The New Tenants

"**The King is** dead," Mrs Scribbins announced as she arrived in the wash house at Iona House on Monday 20th, January, 1936. "The lad as sells papers outside the train station was shouting it. King's face on 'is billboard with a big black border."

"Not totally unexpected," I said, putting the whites into the copper to boil.

"No, suppose not. Sad though. Wonder when the funeral is?" Mrs Scribbins said, pulling out the zinc poss tub from under the sink.

"Don't know but it's bound to be announced. Could even be on the Pathe News," I said, as we filled the tub with hot water.

"Suppose the Prince of Wales is King now," she said.

"Yes he will be. King Edward VIII," I said, having heard the news bulletin on the wireless earlier.

"Popular prince 'e was, 'e'll need to get 'imself a wife now," Mrs Scribbins said.

"I just can't imagine him settling down. He's always been very popular. 'The darling' of society I've heard him described as," I said, sorting the clothes into piles.

"'E 'as that. Proper ladies man. Quite likes 'em married an all, so I'm told," Mrs Scribbins added, starting to poss the first load.

"So I've heard," I said.

A letter arrived for me from Bonny.

The Nurses Home,
Royal Victoria Infirmary,
Newcastle upon Tyne.

January 21st, 1936.

Dear Bettina,

I've been making a few enquiries and Dr Spencer Thistlethwaite does not have a brother or a cousin practising medicine.
He is no longer engaged to the nurse in my crowd. She broke it off as she suspected he was two-timing her. He had the cheek to ask for the ring back as it had, supposedly, been his grandmother's. It was five diamonds, very pretty and she threw it at him. She said he had to grovel around on all fours looking for it and I have a feeling she enjoyed that.
He still works at the Morgan and the Infirmary in Ransington and a friend of mine who works there(the Morgan) say he has asked her out. Now there's a surprise!!!!!

Hope all is well with you and Adam. Is he back in America? Studying hard. Feet still killing me. Went to pictures last week and saw 'Bride of Frankenstein' – frightened the life out of me.
Love,

Bonny. xxxxx

Dr Thistlethwaite was certainly a 'ladies man' and no mistake. I began to wonder if it would end in tears – preferably his.

Sitting with Hilda in her cottage a few days later with Pip and Logan beside me, she confided that her new neighbours were proving so difficult she feared she may have to move house.

"The cottage down at Willow Farm is empty and I've enquired with Albert Dixon about renting it. Willow Farm is not so convenient but I don't think I can stand this much longer."

"Oh Hilda, things must be bad," I exclaimed.

I knew about the borrowing but wondered if something else was going on.

"It's the violence," she said, pouring us another cup of tea.

By coincidence something crashed against the party wall and a man's voice raised in temper could be heard.

"See what I mean," Hilda said, adding, "every day this goes on."

A woman screamed. Further shouting from the man then a child crying. A door slammed, then it all went quiet. We listened, but other than the hiss of the coals on the fire, there was silence.

Leaving the dogs with Hilda I knocked on the front door of Groat Cottage; not feeling at all brave, but sensing a child may be in danger.

A young girl, whom I recognised, opened the door.

"Hello Em," I said to this ragged child with matted hair and whose dirty face was now streaked with tears.

She just stared at me.

"Is your mam in?" I asked

She shook her head indicating no.

"Is your dad in?" was my next question.

"Gone on 'is bike," she replied.

"Then where is your mam?" I asked.

Em did not answer but took my hand and led me through the cottage. I tried not to breathe in the dirty stench of the place which was foul, or look at the filthy mess everywhere. I felt my shoes sticking to the tacky floor.

Standing in the back yard I looked around for Em's mam. The yard appeared to be empty.

"But where is your mam?" I asked gently.

Em pointed to the coal-house which was padlocked.

I knocked on the coal-house door and asked, "Are you in there Em's mam?"

There was no answer. I then heard a cough and a sob.

"Speak to me if you can and I will get you out of there," I said through the door.

"Yes," came the reply. Just one word, quietly spoken.

"Don't let 'er out miss, please. Me dad'll just give 'er a good 'iding if you do," pleaded a frightened Em.

"What's she doing in there anyway?" I asked, trying not to show my anger.

"Always locks 'er in there when 'e's upset. She's always upsettin' 'im. Upsets 'im all the time she does," Em explained.

"Where's he gone? Where's the key?" I asked.

"Work I think. 'e'll 'av taken the key. Allus takes the key," she answered.

"Then when will he be back?" I asked, not quite believing what I was hearing.

"Dunno," she replied.

"Right then Em, I will get your mother out of there. This is cruel," I said.

Em looked worried and said, "'e's not gunna be 'appy."

I walked along to the 'Shoulder of Mutton' and found Jim, the landlord of the pub and of Groat Cottage. I quietly explained the situation to him.

"What, that can't be right. Andy Gibson drinks in here and always pays his rent on time," a shocked Jim said.

"Well I really don't want to debate this Jim. Andy Gibson's wife is locked in the coal-house, he's taken the key and we need to free her," I said, hoping I didn't sound too bossy.

Jim found a crow-bar and together we went to the back yard of Groat Cottage.

*

The lock was quickly broken and a frightened, pregnant woman emerged shaking with cold and fear.

The cottage was too filthy to sit in so I collected Pip and Logan from Hilda's then took Em and her mother over to Providence House; quickly explaining to Agatha why I had brought them.

"Would you like to take a bath Mrs Gibson wash all that coal dust off, Em can have one too if she wants?" I asked.

Em and her mother took some time to discuss whether or not they would like a bath then Em said, "'ave you got any of them nice smelly bath salts?"

I replied, "Yes, lavender, use some if you wish."

"All right then, we'll 'av a bath," they agreed.

"Shall I look for some clean clothes for you whilst you have your bath?" I asked.

"That would be very kind miss, very kind I'm sure. Very kind of yu," Em's mother said.

Agatha found them both a large paper carrier bag into which they could put their dirty clothes and, after showing them to the bathroom I went to look for some suitable underwear and a skirt and jumper each.

When they were bathed and wearing clean clothes we offered them soup and bread which they accepted and ate hungrily.

"I'm Bettina and this is Agatha," I said, then I asked Em's mother her name.

"Em," she replied, adding, "I'm big Em she's little Em."

"Didn't you used to live two doors down from Esther in Ransington?" I asked.

"Yes, with me sister. We came 'ere when me 'usband got work at the airfield what's bein' built," she replied.

"When is your baby due?" I asked, trying to show a friendly interest.

"About two months I think. But I'm goin' back to me sisters to 'av it," she replied.

"I think I met your sister. Isn't she having a baby too?" I asked.

"She is," said little Em, "and it's me dad's an all."

Agatha's jaw visibly dropped and I was glad to be sitting down.

"*What!* He's the father of *both* babies?" I responded, trying not to sound too shocked.

"Yeh, they takes it in turns to sleep in 'is bed. Says 'e's married to both of em but in fact 'e's not married to either – not legal like," little Em calmly stated.

I couldn't quite believe what I was hearing and I could see

that Agatha was visibly shocked.

"Don't you mind?" I asked big Em.

"Not really," was her reply, adding "but I don't like the coal hole."

I didn't know what else to say other than, "Why do you put up with it?"

"Nowhere else to go miss," big Em replied.

They had finished their soup so I asked big Em, "What do you want to do now? We could call the police. Your husband shouldn't lock you in the coal-house, it's against the law."

"No thanks miss. We'll go 'ome if yu don't mind," she said.

Carrying their paper carrier bags big Em and little Em left Providence House, crossed the road and walked home to Groat Cottage; to a life of violence and no education for little Em.

I went to the bathroom to collect the bath towels for the wash but they were nowhere to be found. The jar of Yardley's lavender bath salts had now gone and Agatha's Brown Windsor soap had 'walked'.

The large paper carrier bags had come in handy for their 'stash' I thought whilst washing out the bath. Funnily enough I didn't mind as I appreciated just how much I had, whilst they had so little. However I was relieved to find they had taken their dirty clothes with them.

Agatha was making a pot of tea when I went down to the kitchen.

"Quite a situation," she said.

"Quite a situation," I agreed, handing her the calamine lotion.

"What's this for?" she asked.

"Flea bites, you may find you need it. I know I do," I answered.

14

Rose

A **bitter cold north** east wind blew on Monday 2nd March, 1936, a wind sharp enough to slice through the strongest of top coats.

Enquiries had kept coming in for 'Lingerie Chic' and the order book was full. Agatha and I were both surprised at the demand for our lingerie in both red and black; sometimes ordered by the débutantes unbeknown to their mothers!

Sleet pounded the yard at the back of the washhouse as I helped Mrs Scribbins with the massive amount of laundry we now had at Iona House.

I could see she wasn't herself, so I casually asked, "Something on your mind Mrs Scribbins?"

"Well yes, Bettina, there is. Hime that worried and not sure whether to give up me little volunteering job at the Morgan," she replied.

"But I thought you enjoyed it," I said.

"Oh I do, I really do and Mrs Trevelyan is very kind, so kind. She's called Rose. Such a lovely name and it suits 'er 'cause she's gentle, been hever so good to me she 'as," said Mrs Scribbins.

"Then what's bothering you?" I asked, aware that she was worried about something.

"She's asked me to do the library trolley instead of sweets

Circlet of Gold

and magazines 'cause somebody's off. She, Mrs Trevelyan that is, said that hime so reliable and can I do it," she answered.

I immediately realised why there was a problem. Mrs Scribbins had told me, some time ago, that she couldn't read or write.

"When is it, the library trolley round?" I asked.

"Wednesday evenings, 7 o'clock when the visitors 'av gone," she answered.

"Then why don't we do it together?" I suggested.

"Would you Bettina, are you sure it's not putting you to too much trouble?" she said.

"No trouble at all. The boys are older now and I'm sure they'll be well behaved for Vera. I'll pick you up Wednesday six fifteen," I said to a now visibly more cheerful Mrs Scribbins.

*

Mrs Rose Trevelyan was, as Mrs Scribbins had described, gentle and charming. She took us into a small stock room where the library books were stored, then quietly and patiently, explained about the different genres of books and how to issue the library tickets to the patients.

"The library round should take about an hour if you start the moment the visitors leave," she said.

Mr Trevelyan, whom I had not met before, although Mrs Scribbins had, marched into the small room. I detected that Rose immediately became tense and distracted.

"What do you think you are doing woman?" he said loudly to her in a complaining tone.

"I'll only be a moment more," was her nervous reply.

"Hurry up, hurry up and try to redeem yourself woman, I haven't got all night." He almost spat the words at his wife, whilst leering at me through his pince-nez.

Mr Trevelyan then bristled his moustache and asked, "And who's this new filly, good fetlocks by jove?"

"This is Miss Bettina Dawson, Arnold dear, she will be accompanying Mrs Scribbins this evening," Rose explained.

"Miss Dawson, Miss Dawson. Knew a Major Dawson, army, Third Rifles, any relation?" he asked me whilst moving rather too close for comfort and showering me with his spittle as he spoke in short bursts.

"I don't think so sir," I answered, trying to back away which was impossible in such a small room.

"Damn fine soldier, damn fine, alus waited until he saw the whites of their eyes afore he shot 'em," he reminisced.

As they left the room I noticed Mr Trevelyan give Rose a sharp dig with his fist between her shoulder blades whilst muttering and complaining continuously.

"I wouldn't want to be married to 'im. Poor Rose I feels quite sorry for 'er I do," said Mrs Scribbins, adding, "'e's alus the same."

"Mad as a box of frogs and nasty with it, if you ask me," I said, having gained the impression that I had just met a most unpleasant man.

I enjoyed taking the mobile library around the four wards and several single rooms with Mrs Scribbins. Some patients were 'long stay', usually having had orthopaedic operations and they very much looked forward to the library trolley.

"It must be lovely to be able to read a book," Mrs Scribbins said, one evening on our journey home.

"How about I teach you? Then when you can read a bit I think they run proper classes at the Womens Institute," I suggested.

By the end of March Mrs Scribbins could recognise some simple words and had begun taking an interest in the titles of the books.

"I'm starting at reading class next week," she excitedly told me one Tuesday as she ironed her way through a pile of clothes.

At the commencement of our library round the first Wednesday in April Rose Trevelyan asked, "May I prevail upon you, Mrs Scribbins and Miss Dawson, to perform an extra duty this evening?"

Of course we said yes, thinking it would be a volunteering task.

"Mr Trevelyan and I have been called to a meeting in Matron's office at 7:45pm and I usually take a cup of coffee to Dr Thistlethwaite in the operating theatre office about that time. He is the anaesthetist and calls to see his patients on a Wednesday evening, in readiness for the surgical operating list on Thursday morning," she explained.

We both said we would be happy to take Dr Thistlethwaite a cup of coffee.

"He likes it milky with one sugar," Rose said, smiling serenely and adding, "such a brilliant doctor, works so hard."

At the end of the library round Mrs Scribbins, who now enjoyed reading the titles, packed the books away.

Following the detailed instructions from Mrs Trevelyan I took the milky coffee with one sugar along to the operating theatre office, expecting to find Dr Thistlethwaite- no one was there.

I put the coffee on the desk and then, wondering where he was, went to look for him.

Knowing not to enter the operating theatre, as it was

a clean area where no one was allowed wearing outdoor clothing, I knocked on the door to the next room. The signing on this door read 'anaesthetic room' but there was no reply so I knocked again; still no reply.

Knocking for the third time, I opened the door just enough to pop my head around.

Dr Thistlethwaite was sitting on a stool fiddling with the anaesthetic machine. The distinct impression he gave was that of inhaling the anaesthetic as he had the black rubber mask over his nose and mouth.

Eventually I caught his attention and he looked up and directly at me. His usually handsome face was now florid with a slightly stuporous expression; quite unlike his usual suave, confident self.

Momentarily I stood transfixed, then simply said, "Your coffee is in the office doctor."

On our journey back to Mrs Scribbins flat she said, "Oh Bettina, the library volunteering is the best thing hever. I'm really looking forward to reading a book."

"I'm so pleased you are learning to read Mrs Scribbins," I said, in what I hoped was an encouraging tone.

"'Ave you seen Judge Ian's new car?" she asked.

"No, I've been over at Providence House most days. Agatha and I are busy with our underwear business, really busy, and we are pleased to be busy.

"Hever so flash it is. Bright blue. I think Percy said it were a Riley Bird. I think that's what 'e called it," she said, then added, "me and Iris, well we think Ian is 'avin' one of them mid life crisisis, mind you 'e looks quite the part drivin it."

"What part's that?" I naively asked.

"Heligible widower, that's what part," Mrs Scribbins said.

Arriving back at Iona House, although I hadn't mentioned it to Mrs Scribbins, I couldn't erase the memory from my mind of Dr Thistlethwaite sniffing anaesthetic. I decided to write to Bonny to express my concerns.

Iona House,
Ransington.

March 31st, 1936.

Dear Bonny,

I hope you are well and the thought of your exams looming is not too daunting for you. I have every confidence you will pass with flying colours.
Mrs Scribbins and I now volunteer with the library trolley at the Morgan and when I took Dr Thistlethwaite his coffee I'm sure I saw him taking a whiff of anaesthetic.

Is the engagement still off between him and the nurse you know? By the way Ada was in the Burside chemists the other day and Frank is wearing an engagement ring. Five diamonds which her fiancé says was his grandmother's ring. That is according to Maureen who is the shop assistant there.
The boys are settled at school and the triplets are on the move and into everything.

Good luck with your exams.

Love,

Bettina. xxx

A short letter arrived by return of post.

Nurses Home,
RVI

April 2nd, 1936.

Dear Bettina,

Quick note as I'm up to my eyes. You are probably right. He is a 'wrong un' and no mistake. The anaesthetic of choice for sniffing is called cyclopropane. I heard of an anaesthetist once who used to release a valve on the machine and have a sniff in the middle of an operation. Fell off his stool and broke his arm – stupid b...r! It wasn't at this hospital.
I hope Frank doesn't marry Dr T.
Must fly,

Love,

Bonny xxx

'Hardly likely.' I thought, as he's already married. However I wouldn't put anything past this good looking doctor who seemed to have women falling at his feet.

15

The Date

Easter was always great fun at Iona House and in 1936 more so than ever. The triplets were crawling everywhere and now that Claudette was four and a half and Rory three and a half Vera and Angus had made the decision that a governess would be employed; the morning room would become a school room.

Dr Moshe and Dr Anna were consulted about educating Rory who was deaf.

Claudette had always acted as his interpreter but his parents realised that he needed to learn to communicate independently.

The School For The Deaf insisted that their pupils learnt to lip read and signing was discouraged. Moshe had a cousin in Poland named Jakub who was a trained teacher and had some experience with teaching deaf children. Life in Poland was becoming increasingly difficult for Jewish people and Jakub had already made the decision to leave; he would be arriving in England the following week. One month's trial period teaching Claudette and Rory was agreed.

Jakub was an extremely good looking young man, aged 25 years, who spoke perfect English. He took up his post as teacher to Claudette and Rory. Mornings were spent teaching Claudette reading and writing whilst time was also spent with Rory who learnt to lip read and sign. Afternoons were given over to nature rambles in the garden and park if the weather was fine, or music lessons which they both loved. If the triplets were taking their afternoon nap Mabel would play her accordion and Jakub his violin. Claudette and Rory both enjoyed playing percussion instruments with Rory favouring the xylophone.

A letter arrived from Ada:-

*Rookery Farm,
Little Laxlet.*

April 21st, 1936.

Dear Bettina,

You are not going to believe this but Ian has asked me to go to the theatre with him next week. I've never been much of a one for the theatre except for the panto. at Christmas, so I'm all of a dither.
I was wondering if I could stay with you at Iona House.
He says he's got a new car but won't tell me what it is. Says he wants to surprise me. I think he is taking me to a Gilbert and Sullivan production, whatever that is!
By the way I've signed up for elocution lessons.

Love,

Ada xxx

Circlet of Gold

I had barely absorbed Ada's news when, the following Sunday, who should come strolling across the back lawn but Ian.

"Hello Bettina," Ian said, "I'm pleased to catch you in as I need to ask your advice."

"Advice from me?" I queried, thinking, 'why on earth would a judge need advice from me?'

"Yes, it's Ada you see. Your friend Ada. I've asked her to accompany me to the theatre and I need your advice," Ian said.

"Fire away," I said, not at all confident I would have all, or any, of the answers.

"What kind of chocolate does Ada like, milk or plain?" he asked.

"Definitely milk," I replied.

"Would Ada prefer to sit in a box, the balcony or the stalls?"

"Not sure but I would say probably the balcony," I said.

"Will she want to go to dinner before or after the theatre?" he said, as a worried expression crossed his face.

So I decided to ask him a question.

I then said, "So what is really bothering you Ian?"

"Do you think I'm too old for her?" he blurted out.

"Twenty years is nothing if you care about each other," I said, in what I hoped was an encouraging voice.

His hair, now touched with grey, gave this handsome man a distinguished air and I could well see why Ada was attracted to him.

To reassure him further I then added, "You really shouldn't worry too much. Just be yourself and have a lovely evening. It will be an opportunity to get to know each other better.

I'm sure you'll have a great time," whilst thinking, 'I wonder how Ada's elocution lessons are coming along?'

Ian seemed to relax and said, "Would you like to see my new acquisition, it's on the front drive?"

"Certainly would," I replied, following him around the side of the house to the front.

"What do you think Bettina?" he said, pointing to a brand new blue Riley Kestrel with a black soft top.

"*Wow*, it's just beautiful!" I exclaimed.

"Ada doesn't know about the car. I want to surprise her on Friday. I gather she will be staying with you so I'll collect her about 5pm if that's okay. I think we should have something to eat before the theatre. The Metropole put on a passable theatre supper, I'll book a table," he said, obviously feeling anxious about his evening with Ada.

"Bye Ian, and please, *please* stop worrying," I reassured him.

*

Early afternoon the following Friday Ada arrived. She had travelled by train from Burside having negotiated a half day's leave which she had confidently assured Miss Dent, her boss, was due to her.

The tailor's dummy in the tower room was perfect for hanging Ada's simple dark blue velvet dress. We draped her new lace underwear and silk stockings over the back of an arm chair. The shoes she had brought were also new, navy blue suede with a higher Louis heel than I'd seen Ada wear before. I lent her my cream cashmere stole, which had been my birthday gift from Adam, just in case the evening turned chilly.

Circlet of Gold

I noticed Ada seemed tense as I popped a freshly laundered lace edged handkerchief into her cream clutch bag.

"Why don't you have a bath, it'll relax you and I'll make us a cuppa?" I suggested.

"A double brandy would relax me more," she replied, walking towards the bathroom.

"No alcohol before you meet Ian," I said.

"Okay granny," she laughingly responded.

By 5pm Ada was looking radiant. The blue velvet dress, skimming over her hips and thighs, suited her perfectly. Her dark brown wavy hair cascaded around her face and bounced on her shoulders, just touching the V neck of her dress which flattered her décolletage and bust.

Vera, carrying a perfume spray, came into the bedroom to see Ada before she left for her date with Ian. A spray of 'Arperge' completed the ensemble.

"I don't think I've ever seen her looking so lovely," Vera said as Ada left.

"I know," I agreed, adding "and they seem quite smitten with each other."

We watched Ian and Ada drive off in the blue Riley Kestrel for their first evening together.

I did hope Ian would be feeling more relaxed about the age difference and that Ada would stop worrying about the pronunciation of her vowels.

I'd even heard her practising *'How... now... brown... cow'* in the bath.

The pre-theatre light supper at the Metropole was delicious: asparagus mornay followed by Peach Melba, accompanied by a perfectly chilled bottle of Chateauneuf-du-pape blanc.

Following supper Ada and Ian then walked the short distance to the Empire theatre, leaving the Riley in the Metropole car park.

The production of the Pirates of Penzance, Ada acknowledged to me later, had been entertaining but that she had enjoyed the chocolates more.

After the theatre Ian and Ada walked leisurely back to the Metropole where they each enjoyed a cocktail by the name of 'Seventh Heaven'. Ian then returned with Ada to Iona House where they sat in the car for a short while and where Ada said, "Thank you Ian, it's been a wonderful evening."

He lent across and kissed her on the lips, a tender kiss between two people at the start of their relationship.

Alighting from the car he then walked around and opened the passenger door for Ada.

Arm in arm they then walked slowly the few paces to the front door.

Here Ian took Ada into his arms and pressed his lips to hers. Her response was immediate; with parted lips they kissed passionately, tongues exploring, hardly breathing. Intense was the emotion of the moment as Ian kissed her neck and throat; his breath on her skin aroused Ada, so much so that she quietly, and without saying a word, took Ian's hand and led him around the side of the house to the back of the property and into the potting shed.

Once inside, with the door closed and only a shaft of moonlight shining through the small skylight window to see by, they continued kissing whilst removing some clothing. So keen was their desire for each other that it only took a moment for Ada's lace French knickers to be discarded; the same for Ian's trousers.

Circlet of Gold

Ada spread the cream cashmere stole onto a large sack of peat compost, her blue velvet dress now around her waist.

They lay together on the mound of peat compost and Ada whispered, "Come on then, let's fuck."

Ian, who had been dreaming since Boxing Day of having sex with Ada did not need to be asked twice, said very little but enjoyed his first ever experience of making love in a potting shed, on a pile of compost by the light of the moon.

Ada's moans of pleasure followed by a slightly subdued shriek of delight, muffled into his shoulder, as they climaxed together reassured Ian that this passionate exchange had delighted her as much as it had him.

Afterwards and now fully dressed they brushed each other down then quietly walked back around the house to the front door.

"Good night Ada," Ian said.

"Good night Ian, thank you again for a lovely evening," Ada said.

"No, thank you," he whispered.

They kissed again, a kiss so gentle, warm and meaningful; a kiss which held the promise of many more.

Ada went into Iona House.

Ian drove home, realising he had fallen in love and that he was the happiest man in the world.

The following morning, I took Ada a cup of tea in bed. I noticed peat compost on the floor and also in my cream cashmere stole.

"Good date then was it?" I asked.

"*Fucking brilliant.* Not sure about the Gilbert and Sullivan though," she replied.

16

A New Quilt

May 1936

Vera appeared on the landing carrying, and looking over the top of, a pile of baby clothes. The triplets Donald, Caelen and Izzadora were now 1year and 5months old.

"I've been meaning to sort out the baby things for ages. Do you happen to know anyone needing clothes for newborns and up to a year?" she asked me.

"I think Ruth, the almoner at the infirmary would. I'm sure the baby things would be most welcome," I replied.

Ruth was genuinely pleased to receive the three bags of hardly worn clothing for young babies and assured me that they would quickly be used.

"Infants often arrive here at the Infirmary in rags or naked. Sister Spinks takes great pride in ensuring that each child has a suitable outfit to go home in when he or she is better," she said.

"I've brought them to the right place then," I said.

Ruth then added, matter of factly, "Sadly, if a child does not recover we always ensure he or she is buried in proper clothing."

'All part of the job', I thought.

I then asked, "Is Sister Spinks still in charge of the children's ward?"

Circlet of Gold

"Yes she is, but it is such a shame, I think she will be leaving us," Ruth replied.

"Leaving!" I exclaimed. "but she is so devoted to her work, so lovely with the children and their relatives. Will she be transferring to a different hospital?"

"No, we are losing her because next year Perdita will be getting married," Ruth explained.

"Married, how wonderful for her. When she leaves it will be a great loss to the Infirmary," I said.

"It certainly will but she is very happy and her fiancé is a fine doctor," Ruth said.

"A doctor," I said, knowing intuitively who it was, then adding "a doctor from here at the Infirmary?"

"Yes, although he does work elsewhere as well. Her fiancé is Dr Thistlethwaite the anaesthetist. You may have met him when your brother was a patient here," was her reply.

Ruth was keen to hear about Ivy and pleased when I told her that she had settled in well at Iona House and now held the position of 'mother's help'.

"Would you happen to know if Sister Spinks is on duty today?" I asked.

"Yes she is and I'm sure she'd be delighted if you called in to say hello," Ruth said.

She thanked me again for the baby clothes. I then left her office and walked the short distance to the children's ward.

It was visiting time and I was pleased to see that all the children had visitors at their bedside. Sister Perdita Spinks was sitting at her highly polished desk in the centre of the ward working out the off-duty for her team of nurses whilst simultaneously keeping an eye on her patients and their visitors.

It was a given on the children's ward that, during visiting time, the nurses took the opportunity to enjoy a quick cuppa in the kitchen; usually sitting on the milk crates behind the kitchen door. Should Sister Spinks require any of them she would ring a small desk bell. However, this was not always the case, as some ward sisters insisted that their nursing team cleaned and polished the bed pans or tidied the linen cupboards while the visitors were in.

As I approached the desk her head was dipped so all I could see was her frilly nurses cap on top of her chestnut curls. She then lifted her pretty face to me and smiled in welcome. Her peat brown eyes danced with happiness but I could see that her hands were ring free.

"Hello," I said, "I've just dropped a few things off with Ruth and she said to pop in and say hello."

"How are John and Ivy?" she asked, offering me the chair beside her.

I was amazed at how she remembered the names of all the children.

"They are both doing really well," I replied.

"Good," she said, adding, "I'm so pleased and grateful you took Ivy under your wing."

"A little bird told me that congratulations are in order," I said quietly.

A blush flushed her cheeks.

"Yes it's true, I can't quite believe it myself. Of course I'm not allowed to wear my engagement ring when I'm on duty," Perdita said quietly.

"That's a shame, I would have loved to have seen it," I said.

"Well you can," she said, unbuttoning the top button of

her uniform and pulling out a fine gold chain on which hung a ring.

"Oh, how lovely is that!" I quietly exclaimed, adding, " five diamonds, very much 'on trend' and fashionable at the moment so they say."

"I know," she said. "but it's not new. It was my fiancés grandmother's engagement ring. She was a nurse and when she heard that Spencer was to marry a nurse she insisted that we have the ring."

"That is so lovely," I said, whilst thinking what a cheating, lying bastard Spencer Thistlethwaite was. Already married and now with two fiancées.

We said our goodbyes and I added that I hoped she would be very happy. A sentiment I knew would not come to fruition.

My sewing for 'Lingerie Chic' had taken up so much of my time that I was really missing my quilt making.

As a treat to myself I had decided to make a quilt for my bed at Providence House and I knew, due to time constraints, it would need to be a simple pattern.

Adam's cousin Jenny, with whom I had regular correspondence, suggested a simple nine patch design.

Woolworths had a good selection of fabric but not quite what I was looking for. I'd heard about a new fabric/haberdashery shop which had opened in Ransington by the name of Stockwells; I decided to visit it and was not disappointed. This small shop was a true treasure trove of all things stitching.

Shelves piled high with bolts of cotton fabric padded the walls. Wooden, glass fronted, display cases containing reels of thread in a multitude of colours. Scissors, in all sizes, hung on the back wall; tape measures, pins, needles, tailors' dummies and much, much more. This was going to be an hour of heaven for me – a full hour of self indulgence, just by being there in this little shop which smelled of new cloth.

The shop assistant was charming and together we selected nine different cotton fabrics. Some plain, some patterned, but all toning, in shades of blue on white or white on blue. With my purchases carefully wrapped in brown paper and tied with string I drove home feeling an excitement so intense that only another quilter would understand.

Mrs Scribbins was just finishing the ironing when I arrived back at Iona House.

"Fancy a cuppa Bettina?" she asked, putting the kettle on the hot plate.

"Do I ever say no?" I replied.

"Well," she said, "I'm starting at me reading class this week."

"How exciting," I responded. "you must be looking forward to it."

"I am that, and do you know what I fancy reading more than anything?" she said.

"I have no idea," I answered.

"Little Women, yes Little Women, that's what I fancy," Mrs Scribbins said with enthusiasm.

"It's a good story, I'm sure you'll enjoy reading it," I encouraged.

She scalded the teapot.

"'ave you 'eard about Hian?" she asked.

"Heard *what* about Ian?" I cautiously enquired.

"Only 'ad your friend Ada visiting, up at 'ampton 'ouse

with 'im. Esther told me," she said, pouring boiling water onto the tea leaves.

I did, of course, know that Ada had visited Hampton House for lunch on Saturday, but couldn't understand how Esther knew as she only cleaned there on week days.

"It was the bed what giv 'em away. Smelled of perfume when Esther changed the sheets; wasn't the same as what Dora used," she said, pouring the tea.

"Really," I said, in what I hoped was a non-committal tone.

"Then there was the two long dark 'airs on the pillow case," she added, sipping her tea.

I said nothing but thought, 'some lunch that must have been!'

"Then there was the bath," Mrs Scribbins said, offering me a biscuit.

"The bath?" I repeated, accepting a rich tea.

"Yes dead give away, two bath towels in the basket. They must 'ave 'ad a bath together," she said.

"Mmm, but what makes Esther think it was Ada, it might not have been," I said thinking this remark might stop the speculation.

"Oh it was definitely Ada," Mrs Scribbins announced. "Most definite. Stanley Handyside was dropping some plants off in 'is van on Saturday about 5 o'clock. Took 'is mother with 'im, for the run out like, lovely hevening it was."

'Bad timing,' I thought, 'so much for Ada's visit being a secret.'

"Has they harrived oo should be drivin out of those helectrified gates but Hian and Ada in that new blue car of 'is," she said, adding, "well of course Hedna told me and quite surprised she was. So when Esther said a lady had been there on Saturday, well we just put two and two together."

"Are you surprised Mrs Scribbins?" I asked.

"Not in the least Bettina, and good luck to 'em I say. 'opes they finds 'appiness together. She could do a lot worse for 'erself, a lot worse. Good luck to 'em."

"I echo that Mrs Scribbins. Good luck to them," I said, as we raised and clinked our tea cups together.

17

Her Ladyship

June 1936

"**There's going to** be an auction up at The Manor," Agatha said one morning as we were cutting out garments in the sewing room at Providence House.

"That sounds interesting. When is it?" I said.

"Saturday June 27th," Agatha replied, "I've sent for the catalogue. It should be a good day out."

"The Manor is a fabulous old house," I said, "well it's much more than just a house, I think most of it is Jacobean but Lady Rachael did once tell me that there are parts which are medieval."

"Charlie will be coming up for the weekend, she hasn't seen The Manor, except from the road, so it'll be a treat for her," Agatha said.

"I've only been inside once," I said, "that was when Ada and I brought Rachael home after the cricket match. We didn't have the opportunity to look around on that sad occasion, but it is vast."

"At least twenty five bedrooms I've been told and a huge stable block," Agatha said.

"I don't suppose you've heard anything on the grapevine about Rachael. You know, how she is or even if she is still alive?" I asked.

"Not sure, but Mary on the switchboard in the police

station at Burside took a message about extra traffic on the roads approaching The Manor. The organisers have requested help from the police to direct it on the day of the auction, and she said she got the impression that Lady Rachael had died. Maureen in the chemists, she's Mary's friend, told me that," Agatha said.

"How are you and Charlie getting on?" I asked.

"Just fine. We are lovers now, perhaps you'd guessed," she replied with a twinkle in her eye.

"Well I didn't see any point in waiting for Frank. She's definitely engaged and the wedding is planned for next Spring," Agatha continued.

"Do I remember you saying the engagement ring had been her fiancés grandmother's? I tentatively asked.

"Yes that's what I was told," Agatha said.

"Don't suppose she was a nurse, this grandmother?" I added.

"No idea, why do you ask?" Agatha said.

"Oh! Just someone I met recently has just become engaged to a doctor and the ring was his grandmother's. The old lady had been a nurse," I casually said.

"I'm sure Maureen will know. I'll ask her the next time I'm in the chemists," Agatha said.

"Are you thinking of buying anything in particular at the auction?" I asked.

"Not sure what I want. We just want to go for the day out and to see inside The Manor. Charlie reckons we'll know what we want when we see it," Agatha said.

"Coo-ee, coo-ee," Hilda called as she popped her head around the sewing room door.

"Just thought I'd call with the news," she said, then adding,

"Oh I do like those cami-knickers, oh the insert of lace in the neckline is beautiful. Are they for one of your debs?"

"They are, but what is your news, hope it's good?" I said.

The thought of news was rather distracting so Agatha and I decided that we had cut out sufficient for the time being.

"It is, it's the best ever news," Hilda said, bursting with excitement. "The tenants have gone from Groat Cottage."

"That most certainly is good news, when did they go?" Agatha asked.

"Just last week. Jim has had to have the whole cottage fumigated, alive with fleas it was. A lot of stuff had to be thrown away and some was missing," Hilda said.

"Missing, do you mean stolen?" I asked.

"No, Jim thinks they chopped up the table for fire wood. The chairs and sideboard as well. Good job Louisa's treadle sewing machine is over here," Hilda said.

"I reckon Jim'll be well out of pocket," Agatha said.

"Well that's the funny thing. Andy Gibson always paid his rent on time so there are no arrears but he was a real bad bugger – pardon me swearing," said Hilda.

"Hilda, that's the first time I've ever heard you swear!" I exclaimed.

"I know, I'm sorry but he was," she said.

Ada was our next caller. She looked radiant and had come with news that she had handed in her notice at the police station.

"It's getting awkward working with Emrys," she said.

Agatha, Hilda and myself nodded and collectively murmured. "Mmmm." Ada had our full attention.

"Didn't take it well, me dumping him," she said.

"Did you do it gently?" Hilda asked.

"Well sort of," she replied.

"What do you mean, well sort of?" I asked.

"Well, when he said, 'shall we go to the pictures Saturday night?' I just said, 'no you're dumped,'" was Ada's matter of fact answer.

"Just like that?" Agatha said.

"Yes, just like that. There's no easy way to dump someone so I'm always direct. That way they definitely understand you mean what you say," she explained.

'No chance of dubiety with the Ada method of dumping,' I thought.

Pip and Logan were due for their walk so Ada and I left Agatha and Hilda chatting while we took a leisurely stroll in the sunshine.

As always Little Laxlet looked as pretty as a picture and the scent of roses and honeysuckle filled the air.

"Looks as though it's serious with you and Ian then?" I enquired.

"It is, I like him loads," she said with a wistful look on her face.

"Adam says he'll be home at the end of the year," I said.

"Where is he now?" Ada asked.

"He was in America, then he went to Germany then to France for some reason, then London and now back to America. All to do with his studies and also his job with Nick Van der Linden," I said.

Passing the telephone box reminded me of when Adam and I had our first kiss.

"That's where we had our first kiss," I said, nodding to the telephone box.

"Oh that is so romantic. Is he a good kisser?" Ada asked.

"He certainly is and I miss him such a lot," I said.

"I don't know how you stand the separation," Ada said.

"It's not easy, but I love him and I'm prepared to wait," I said.

"I'm not," Ada said.

"Not what?" I said.

"Prepared to wait," she said.

"Really," I said, wondering what she was going to reveal next.

"Want to know a secret?" she asked.

"Of course," I replied.

"Ian and me, well we're in love and I've given up on the elocution," she said.

"Good and good," I said, giving Ada a hug to show how happy I felt for her.

"Is he a good kisser?" I then asked because I felt she wanted me to.

"Bloody fantastic, and we have had some brilliant Saturdays up at Hampton House," she said with enthusiasm.

"Yes your cover was blown when Stan and his mother spotted you and Ian leaving," I said.

Not fazed by this Ada then said, "Ian is incredibly highly sexed you know.".

'Then you should be perfect for each other.' I thought.

"We usually manage to fit in three fucks at each visit," was Ada's matter of fact description.

'Energetic Saturdays.' I thought.

"We usually have a bath together as well. He has a huge bath and a huge cock..." she said, dreamily.

I was pleased we were on the outskirts of the village and there was no one else about.

"Have you ever had a bath with a man Bettina?" Ada asked.

"No, in fact I've never shared a bath with anyone," I answered.

"Then you should, the next time your Adam's home. Plenty of bubbles covering your tits gets them all excited. Then there's all that mystery of what's under the water. All that slipping, sliding and feeling about," she said, adding, "ooh … it's lovely."

In my mind I tried to imagine it.

"We usually have sex on the bathroom floor, after our bath, wrapped in big fluffy bath towels," Ada said.

"So it's looking serious then," I said.

"Certainly is," she said, adding, "but there's one thing I'm absolutely sure about."

"What's that then?" I asked.

"There is no way on earth I would be willing to live in Hampton House. I'm sure that bloody Dora haunts the place. It's creepy," Ada said with feeling.

"Is Ian aware how you feel?" I asked.

"Not yet, but Seth and Edwin will be home from school in a couple of weeks and we'll tell them about us then," she replied, adding "then I'll break it to Ian about not living in Dora's fucking mansion."

"Do you think marriage will be on the cards?" I enquired.

"Definitely, once his boys are told," she said with confidence.

"Has Ian actually proposed?" I tentatively enquired.

"Not yet but he will. Would you make my wedding dress and some of those gorgeous silk undies for my honeymoon?"

"Of course I will but I'll need a bit of notice. A wedding dress can't be rushed," was my reply.

*

Jim was standing outside the 'Shoulder of Mutton' just shaking hands with and saying goodbye to a man whom Ada recognised as being a surveyor from the council.

"Hello girls, how are you both?" Jim smilingly asked.

"Fine thanks Jim," we said.

"Any sign of a tenant for Groat Cottage?" I asked.

"Yes and I'm having water installed and a small bathroom built behind the kitchen. That was the surveyor," Jim said.

"Will you be going to the auction at The Manor?" Ada asked.

"Indeed I will. Those Gibsons from Ransington used anything and everything made of wood for fuel," he said.

"There should be some good furniture, it's viewing the day before," I said.

"Hope it's not too expensive, see you there," said Jim, as we waved goodbye and walked back to Providence House.

Agatha was just finishing inserting an ecru lace panel into the front of a pair of pink cami-knickers.

Ada was taking a decidedly detailed look at our stock. "With a view," she said, "for honeymoon wear."

Agatha and I exchanged a glance.

"Oh! I love these. These are the best I've ever seen, ever!" Ada exclaimed pointing to several items we had put to one side for a special order.

"Who did you say they are for?" she asked.

"Well to be honest," Agatha said, "we are not exactly sure. A mystery client."

"Confidentiality is very important in our business," I said. "All I can tell you is that a Mrs Brown telephoned the order through with her 'Ladyship's' measurements and the order. French knickers, cami-knickers, two slips and a nightdress."

Ada was looking in the 'Lingerie Chic' order book.

"AHAH!" she exclaimed loudly, "here it is, here's the mystery lady. No name just an address.

Her Ladyship. c/o Mrs Brown,
Fort Belvedere,
Surrey."

Agatha and I had such a full order book, mostly from titled people we didn't take much notice of the address until it was time to despatch the garments.

All three of us then realised who 'Her Ladyship' was.

"Her Ladyship, what a joke. Thinks she'll be our queen when she marries King Edward. Personally I can't see that **ever** happening. She might get to marry him but she'll **never** be queen," Ada remarked, adding, "anyway she's still married to her second husband."

"Ada," I said firmly, "I need to stress the importance of confidentiality, if any details of 'Lingerie Chic' clients are made public then we'll be finished."

"I understand that, of course I understand but I still want the same as her *so called* Ladyship," Ada said with a touch of petulance in her voice.

"Which colours will you be wanting Ada?" asked Agatha, pen and order book in her hands.

"Virginal white for my wedding day, what else. Then black with red ribbons for the honeymoon," Ada said.

"Black with red ribbons?" queried a wide eyed Agatha.

"If it's good enough for her so called fucking Ladyship then it'll do nicely for me," Ada said.

"Do you have anything in mind for your wedding dress?" I asked.

"Not yet but I soon will have," she replied.

"Remember Ada, confidentiality," I gently reminded her.

"Don't worry I get it. No confidentiality – no wedding dress. I'm not risking that by letting out secrets about the King and his mistress. No way," she said with conviction.

Reflecting later on that conversation I truly believed Ada would keep the secret – well at least until after her wedding.

18

The Auction

It was the middle of June 1936 when the obituary of Lady Rachael Soames appeared in 'The Times'. She had died peacefully in her sleep in a nursing home in Devon. The funeral was to be private.

On Saturday June 27th, 1936 Agatha, Charlie, Hilda and I arrived early for the auction, or dispersal of goods, at The Manor, Little Laxlet.

Viewing of the items had been on the previous day, and judging by the number of people attending the viewing, myself included, I was aware that to arrive early on auction day would be the only way to ensure us a good seat near the front.

At the viewing I had seen three items which were of interest to me. A Victorian mahogany sewing box, two patchwork quilts (together in one lot) and a Lalique compote dish.

Ada and Ian arrived, both looking relaxed and happy, and chose to sit near the back of the room.

We waved, then Hilda said, "I wouldn't wave once the auctions starts or you'll find yourself buying something you don't want."

Much to my surprise I noticed Mr and Mrs Trevelyan enter the room and take seats fairly near to us. Rose Trevelyan noticed me and we smiled in acknowledgement. Within minutes of arriving Mr Trevelyan left his seat and went over to a table on which a large amount of china was displayed. He examined some items through his pince-nez and also used a magnifying glass, his nail brush moustache twitching as he consulted the auction catalogue.

"Which dinner service is it?" he shouted to Rose from across the room.

Looking embarrassed, she went over to him and together they consulted the catalogue and looked at the china.

"Damn it you stupid woman!" was the expletive form in which he addressed Rose; causing several bystanders to turn and look at them.

Keeping her voice low and encouraging him to do the same they finally decided which of the china was of interest to them.

On their way back to their seats Rose stopped to say hello and I introduced her to Hilda, Agatha and Charlie.

"We are here to buy a wedding present for our daughter," Rose said.

"Anything in particular?" I asked.

"There is a fine Shelley dinner service we are hoping to get. My daughter viewed it yesterday but, unfortunately, she is working today so couldn't be here. My husband will bid for it," Rose answered.

Rose Trevelyan then took her seat beside her husband.

I hadn't been aware that she had a daughter; Rose was a private person and never discussed personal matters when we were volunteering.

The enormous room was full, standing room only, and the bidding was brisk.

Ada and Ian bought several pieces of furniture including a

four poster bed. I managed to win the mahogany sewing box and the two quilts but missed out on the Lalique compote dish.

Hilda successfully bid for a bundle of linen.

Agatha and Charlie seemed interested in garden ornaments and bought a marble statue of a goddess.

"She'll look lovely in the garden when the moon shines on her," said Agatha.

"She will that," agreed Charlie, stroking Agatha's arm.

As Hilda and I were leaving to put our items into my car and Agatha and Charlie were waiting in a queue to arrange delivery and pay for theirs, I noticed Dr Thistlethwaite and his pretty dark haired wife, Belinda, in the stable yard, which was in use as a parking area for the auction.

They were bickering loudly whilst loading a large mirror into the boot of his car. I had not seen them in the auction but as the room was so full this was unsurprising.

Mr and Mrs Trevelyan happened to be beside Hilda and me as we walked, with our purchases, into the stable yard and to the car.

"Look Rose, there's Spencer!" Mr Trevelyan exclaimed, digging his wife in the ribs.

"Where?" she said, looking into the crowd.

"Are you blind woman, there, over there," he said crossly, pointing to Dr Thistlethwaite and his wife.

"Oh, so it is. That must be the sister he speaks about. We must try to catch them before they leave. *Yoo-hoo, yoo-hoo*," Rose called, running towards them.

Spencer Thistlethwaite, now with his wife in his car, looked directly at Mrs Trevelyan and drove out of the stable yard at great speed.

Two women were standing beside me and one commented, "Blimey, they were in one hell of a rush."

Her companion said, "Yes, they did seem to be in a hurry. Lovely couple. They are my new neighbours, they'll be rushing home to the baby I suppose."

"That is not accurate madam, allow me to correct you," Mr Trevelyan said, addressing the woman in his usual rude manner.

"What on earth do you mean, you impolite man? Of course I'm not incorrect. Moved in just a few weeks ago, she was a nurse and he is a doctor. So put that in your pipe and smoke it," the woman replied, then briskly walked away.

Mr Trevelyan just stood there with his mouth opening and closing, muttering, "Damned forthright woman, no manners, won't be told."

Ada, packing boxes into the boot of the blue Riley Kestrel, looked stunning in a black and white summer dress with a red silk scarf tying back her long dark brown hair, said "How do you fancy a look around The Manor? Ian's arranging it with the auctioneer."

John and Alfie were playing cricket with Simon Blackwood, who was now old enough to be responsible for them and Mrs Davis, who was not interested in the auction, would be giving them their tea so I was not in a hurry to go home.

"I certainly do," I replied. "I'll just get Hilda, Agatha and Charlie. Is it okay if they come too?"

"Course it is," said Ada.

The Manor, Little Laxlet was an incredibly massive, beautiful property. The Medieval, Jacobean and Georgian parts of the building seemed to merge into each other with ease. We were amazed to be shown a chapel then a ballroom which contained two grand pianos, several huge chandeliers and four sets of French windows which opened out onto a terrace. Room after fabulous room; we walked through periods of history, each owner had increased the size of The Manor in the architectural style of the period.

The twenty five bedrooms, some with an adjoining bathroom, each had a different wooden shield on its oak door, the significance of which the auctioneer told us he was unsure.

Ian asked many questions and when the auctioneer bid us goodbye from under the stone portico entrance he informed us that The Manor was to be sold by sealed bid the following month.

Ada, who was interested in seeing the stables, asked, "Will it be okay if we wander around the stables."

The auctioneer, of course, replied in the affirmative adding, "Mr Hepscot, our equine specialist, is on hand over there should you have any questions."

Hilda and Agatha both admitted to feeling tired following our tour around The Manor so we declined the visit to the stables.

"What an amazing place that would be to live," I said to Hilda, Agatha and Charlie as we drove out of the estate through the deer park.

"You're very quiet Agatha," Charlie said.

"Well yes I know I am and I'm wondering if my mind is playing tricks on me," Agatha said quietly.

"In what way?" I asked.

"You know that Mr and Mrs Trevelyan sitting near us, you

introduced her to us?" Agatha said, adding, "well I think I've met them before."

"I don't know where," I said, "they live in Ransington as far as I know. Where do you think you've met them before?"

"It's only a memory and a blurred one at that, but I think they are Frank's parents," Agatha said.

"What's Frank's last name?" Hilda asked.

"Parsons," Agatha replied.

"Well they are Trevelyan. Are you sure it was them?" I said.

"No I'm not sure, but I think it was them. I recognised his awful voice," Agatha said.

"Come to think of it they were looking for a wedding present for their daughter," Charlie said.

'So they were' I thought, whilst saying, "Strange coincidence" and not mentioning that I'd seen Dr Thistlethwaite and his wife drive away at speed.

Introducing a new topic of conversation I said, "Ian bought masses of furniture today. I wonder where he's going to store it."

"In one of the barns at Rookery Farm, Ada told me that herself," Hilda said.

"They seem captivated with each other," Charlie said.

"I know," said Hilda, adding, "and I think I hear the sound of wedding bells. Am I right Bettina?"

"You are absolutely correct but, as yet, no date has been set. They want to discuss it with Ian's boys first," I said.

"When are his boys home from school?" Agatha asked.

"Two weeks time or thereabouts," I replied.

"Oh good, so not too long to wait. We love a romantic ending, don't we Charlie?" said Agatha.

Circlet of Gold

"You know what they say," said Charlie.

"What do they say?" I asked.

"An old man's darling or a young man's slave, so the saying goes," Charlie said.

"Do you consider Ian old then?" I asked.

"Well he's twenty years older than Ada and that's a big age gap," said Agatha.

"She's certainly his darling," said Hilda, adding, "and he's loaded and generous with it."

"Should work out for them then," I said.

Lots of love and loads of money, we all agreed was a recipe for success.

"Fingers and toes crossed then that it will work out for them," I said.

"Work out, it'll more than work out," Hilda commented.

"How do you mean?" I asked.

"Ada's got him wrapped around her little finger. That's how," she replied.

'Well observed,' I thought.

19

Retribution

July 1936

Ill-natured rain pelted Mrs Scribbins and me as we ran across the car park into the Morgan Endowment Hospital for our volunteering library session.

Mrs Trevelyan did not seem her usual serene self, greeting us with a shrug and a rigid expression.

We commented on the heavy rain but she said nothing in acknowledgement.

"What's wrong Mrs Trevelyan? I don't want to pry but is there anything we can 'elp you with?" Mrs Scribbins asked.

In a voice devoid of expression Rose Trevelyan said, "I have made a catastrophic discovery which I cannot speak about now as we have a duty to the patients."

'She knows,' I thought, 'she's found out that Spencer Thistlethwaite is a married man.'

Mrs Scribbins and I exchanged a concerned look.

I said, "Why don't you go home Mrs Trevelyan? Mrs Scribbins and I can manage here, you are clearly upset."

"Thank you my dear but home would be no refuge for me at the moment as Mr Trevelyan is in such a towering rage this evening. I have no appetite for being in his company," she said sadly.

This disclosure did not surprise me as I had figured out, from his behaviour, that Arnold Trevelyan was a brute and a bully; this revelation from his wife only confirmed my suspicions.

Mrs Trevelyan then asked, "Do you think you both could manage the library round yourselves this evening? I may just stay here in the store room and sort out some books."

"Somethin's very wrong," said Mrs Scribbins, as we pushed the library trolley onto the first ward.

"Certainly is," I confirmed.

The library round went well and Mrs Scribbins told me she was enjoying her reading lessons at the Womens Institute.

We wheeled the trolley back to the storeroom expecting to find Mrs Trevelyan there but the light was out and she had gone.

"There's a note 'ere," Mrs Scribbins said.

It read, 'Feeling unwell, sorry. See you next week.'

"Oh dear, what'll we do about the doctor's coffee?" Mrs Scribbins said, anxiously.

"He'll just have to do without," was my reply.

"Oooo, she wouldn't like that; Rose is always very particular about the doctor's coffee," Mrs Scribbins said, with concern in her voice.

"Well I for one won't be making him coffee," I said firmly; thinking, 'this so called charming doctor is devoid of any charm. In fact he is quite loathsome.'

"I'll make 'is coffee then Bettina, how did Rose say 'e liked it?" Mrs Scribbins offered.

"Milky, one sugar," I said, whilst thinking, *'deadly nightshade and one hemlock.'*

Mrs Scribbins went off to the kitchen to make the coffee and I started packing the books away onto the shelves, expecting her to return by the time I'd finished.

At 8:30pm she still hadn't returned to the store room so I went to search for her in the operating theatre office, thinking she would have found someone to chat to.

Mrs Scribbins was in the operating theatre office, sitting in a chair with a look of pure horror on her face. When she saw me she pointed toward the corridor, any explanation withered on her lips.

As I walked into the corridor and approached the anaesthetic room I saw the blood. Only a small pool, but blood nevertheless, which had seeped under the right hand door.

Taking care not to stand in it I cautiously opened the left hand door a small amount; this proved difficult as Dr Spencer Thistlethwaite was slumped on the floor behind it. However the door opened sufficiently for me to see that his head was badly beaten, his clothing was badly blood stained and he was unconscious or worse.

Following this gruesome discovery I returned to the operating theatre office and helped the traumatised Mrs Scribbins back to the reception area and alerted Matron to the serious situation in the anaesthetic room.

Realising that we could be at the Morgan for some time, as the police had been called and we would be required for questioning, Matron agreed that I may use the telephone in her office to explain to Vera why I had been delayed.

Dr Thistlethwaite was indeed dead. The police Inspector interviewed Mrs Scribbins and myself both separately and together, in Matron's office; asking many questions regarding our movements during the evening.

Circlet of Gold

It was established that Mrs Scribbins had seen the body when she looked for him to tell him his coffee was in the office and that I then found Mrs Scribbins, in a state of shock some short time later. The questions continued and I began to feel we were going around in circles.

At 10:15pm Matron's telephone rang; the call was for the police Inspector.

"Yes. When? Who?" he said into the telephone.

Then turning to me he said, "You and Mrs Scribbins may leave."

"You may leave," Mrs Scribbins repeated several times on our drive home.

"How are you feeling now?" I asked her.

"Bit better now, but what a shock hive 'ad. Never seen henythhin' like it in me life. Never seen so much blood. Never; and 'im with 'is 'ed caved in," she said.

"I wonder what that telephone call was about?" I said.

"Don't know, but it got us out of there and for that hime thankful," she said, obviously relieved.

The telephone call had been to tell the Inspector that a woman had walked into Ransington police station and confessed to the murder of Dr Spencer Thistlethwaite.

"I have killed Dr Thistlethwaite at the Morgan Endowment Hospital," Rose Trevelyan said, placing a Webley revolver on the duty officer's counter.

The desk Sergeant, using two cloths, opened the gun and removed three bullets.

He then asked Rose some questions and filled out a form.

"It was me. I killed him to protect my daughter from a bigamous marriage," she said clearly.

"From what? Protect her from what?" the desk Sergeant repeated.

An ashen-faced Rose was then taken into the interview room to await the return of the Inspector.

"Would you like to make a telephone call, perhaps to your solicitor?" the Sergeant asked, handing Rose a cup of water.

"No thank you. I killed the doctor," she calmly said.

"Do you have anyone you would like me to call. Your husband perhaps?" the Sergeant offered.

The question hung in the air for a while.

Then with a smile, which under any other set of circumstances would have been engaging, Rose said, whilst staring at the police officer with her benevolent blue eyes, "There is absolutely no point officer, you see he is also dead, It is one of the absurdities of life that I too married a bigamist; a bully and a bigamist. He punctured my self-esteem but tonight I have murdered him. You will find my, so called, husband on the kitchen floor of our home. There is little else to add."

Frank, of course, was devastated to hear that her mother had murdered her fiancé and shot her step-father. However, when the truth was revealed that Arnold Trevelyan was a bigamist and Spencer Thistlethwaite was already married she began to have more understanding of her mother's actions.

Sister Perdita Spinks was equally overwhelmed to discover that her husband-to-be was dead. However, being of a stoical personality and a very sensible woman, she came to the conclusion that Rose Trevelyan had done her a favour.

On the morning of the incidents Rose had received a telephone call from a Mrs Bessie Trevelyan, claiming that

Arnold was her husband. When confronted he did not deny this but tried to justify the situation by telling Rose that his marriage to her was one of convenience as Bessie had been making his life unbearable.

Rose Trevelyan, at the time of her marriage to Arnold, was the widow of Byron Parsons, who had been an army officer in the Great War. She had kept his Webley firearm; always loaded but well hidden.

When she discovered that Frank's (Francene's) fiancé was married she took the gun to the Morgan with the intention of shooting him. Perhaps not to kill him, rather to wound him to teach him a lesson.

The visitors were in the wards as Rose, with the gun concealed in her handbag, went in search of Spencer. She found him in the anaesthetic room sniffing a substance from the anaesthetic machine over which he was leaning.

Realising that not only would a gun shot be heard, but that it could also cause an explosion, she picked up a small portable cylinder of oxygen and brought it crashing down on his head – several times.

Rose then calmly walked back to the store room, spoke to Bettina and Mrs Scribbins who then commenced their library round; she then left the hospital alongside the visitors, and caught a bus back to her home.

Arnold Trevelyan was standing in the kitchen about to pour himself a beer when she arrived back at her house.

"I want you to leave immediately," Rose calmly said to him.

"*Leave!* And where do you suppose I would go you stupid bitch?" he snarled.

"I don't care where you go. Go back to your wife," she said, her voice rising.

"*Wife!* You must be joking. She's even more pathetic than you. Women! You're all the same. Stupid, gutless and needy, the lot of you, stupid, gutless and needy, *pathetic the lot of you,*" he repeated laughing; spittle sticking to his nail brush moustache.

He turned away, pouring the beer, not realising that Rose had removed the gun from her handbag and it now pointed directly at him.

His pince-nez fell with him to the ground, as did his beer, when the bullet tore into his chest.

Rose had aimed the gun at his heart but the gun jerked as she pulled the trigger and the bullet lodged near his shoulder. Unbeknown to Rose, Arnold Trevelyan was not dead – merely badly injured.

She immediately left the house and walked to the park with the intention of throwing herself in the lake to drown. Being undecided, she sat for a while in the children's play area, quietly and gently spinning around on the small roundabout, trying to remember the events which had just taken place and singing quietly to herself.

Eventually she made the decision to go to the police station and hand herself and the Webley revolver in. At least that would prevent a miscarriage of justice if someone else was held, charged and possibly convicted of the two crimes.

Spencer's widow, Mrs Belinda Thistlethwaite, inherited the family home; a charming Edwardian property in the leafy suburbs of Ransington. She found she no longer required medication for her 'nerves'; nor had need to wonder where her husband ventured at night. She had been a nurse prior to her marriage and was a curious person. During her marriage to Spencer her curiosity turned, understandably, into suspicion.

The night of his murder Mrs Thistlethwaite had called into the Morgan; entering by a small side door which was rarely used. Her objective was to catch her husband 'in flagrante' with another woman, instead of which she found him slumped on the floor of the anaesthetic room with a serious head injury.

Checking his pulse and ascertaining he was still alive she then calmly opened her husband's Gladstone bag. Removing several glass ampoules containing morphine, which she skilfully opened and, using a small needle, she drew the contents of all of them into a glass syringe.

Taking his left hand in hers she looked for a vein which had not collapsed; this proved difficult as his condition was moribund. Belinda then realised that the way Spencer was slumped, partly on his back with his legs splayed, gave her easy access to the fly opening in his trousers which she quickly unbuttoned. Without hesitation she changed the needle to a longer one and with great speed she injected the contents of the syringe into his groin, the irony of the which did not escape her; she then re-buttoned his fly and closed the Gladstone bag.

Popping the syringe, needles, glass ampoules with their sawn off tops and even the serrated blade she had used to open the ampoules into her jacket pocket, she left as she had entered, by the rarely used side door, taking care not to step into his blood and erasing her finger prints from the doors, as she had done with the Gladstone bag.

On her drive home Belinda stopped the car on a bridge where she dropped the contents from her jacket pocket into the deep, fast flowing river.

Her nanny, who had also been sleeping with her husband, was dismissed immediately following the funeral.

Rose Trevelyan received the death penalty for the murder of Dr Spencer Thistlethwaite.

Arnold Trevelyan eventually recovered from his bullet wound, later to be tried for bigamy.

There were never any flowers placed on Dr Spencer Thistlethwaite's grave but Belinda took to wearing a fresh flower in her dark hair again.

20

An Engagement

September 1936

A **letter arrived for** me with a German stamp; I recognised Adam's handwriting.

Kleinschmidtstraße 712
Heidelberg.

1ˢᵗ September, 1936.

My Darling Bettina,

First I must tell you how much I miss you and that I'm hoping to be back in England for Christmas.
Nick Van der Linden, as you know, has a massive engineering company among other things. He is planning on manufacturing his own packaging for all the components he sends around the USA and other countries also.
Tomorrow I shall be visiting a factory here in Heidelberg to look at printing machinery with a view to Nick's company buying two printing presses and transporting them to America. Other than looking at the printing presses I'm enjoying walking and the weather is good. You and I both enjoy doing a crossword and my challenge to myself this week is to complete one in the German newspaper.

When I leave here I go back to London for a couple of days before sailing for New York.

I love you,

Adam xxx

Germany was becoming increasingly militarised and the Nazi party more powerful by the day. The Pathé News had shown film of the Berlin Olympic Games in August 1936 and Jesse Owens winning four gold medals for America. I felt concerned for Adam especially as our codeword for not being able to be open and frank in our letters was 'crossword'.

In Germany Adam was shocked by the changes he found since his last visit. Jewish businesses had been closed down and there were now limits on travel. Worst of all Jewish people were now denied citizenship and marriage with non-Jewish Germans.

He took a taxi to the printing factory where there was to be a demonstration of the latest printing press by Herr Schneider, the factory owner. Adam spoke perfect German so communication would not be a problem.

The printing press was impressive and perfectly capable of handling all weights of paper, including cardboard.

Adam was then taken to another press where maps were being printed and packed ready for distribution. Various technical details about the printing presses were discussed by the two men then Herr Schneider went into his office to look for a manual to give to Adam. During his absence of approximately ten minutes Adam took the opportunity of having a closer look at the maps. The technician operating the printing press was proud of his work and happy to give

Adam a demonstration. All were the same and of Poland; markings on the maps indicated that they were for use by the German military.

When Herr Schneider returned with the manual Adam expressed his interest in the printing presses and placed an order for two; to be exported to the USA as soon as possible.

"I wonder, do you have any samples of your printing I could take back to show Mr Van der Linden in America?" Adam asked in perfect German, then added, "It would demonstrate the versatility of the presses."

Herr Schneider, so pleased to have taken an order for two printing presses, then gave Adam a selection of leaflets, pamphlets and flyers all promoting the Nazi party in one form or another.

The purchase of the printing presses for Nick was genuine, and part of Adam's role in the American company. A job which was a perfect cover for his work with the British government.

When he returned to London his first task was to report to the department of the Secret Intelligence Service in Whitehall – MI6.

A letter from Ada gave me the news I had been expecting.

Rookery Farm,
Little Laxlet.

10th September, 1936.

Dear Bettina,

Ian has been to see my dad and asked for my hand in marriage. How proper is that!!!!
Of course dad said yes, so now Ian and I are engaged.
The engagement party, Saturday September 26th, will be at our farm with a band, a spit roasted hog and singer.
There'll be loads of food and dancing in the big barn.

No date set yet for the wedding but I'm thinking May next year might be a good month. Gives you time to make my dress which will be floaty and summery – ever so romantic.
I would like you to be my bridesmaid (chief bridesmaid) and I'll be asking Delicia and our Molly to be matron's of honour.
I'm very excited but thought it only fair to tell Ian that there is no way I want to live at Hampton House. He seems okay about it so that's a hurdle over and out of the way.
As yet I don't have an engagement ring but we are going to a posh jeweller in Harrogate on Saturday.

Love,
Ada. xxx

ps Just read through and, in case you were wondering, it's the hog that will be spit roasted and not the singer. Ha Ha – bet you can tell I'm excited.

The ring Ian and Ada chose together was Edwardian and fabulous; the central diamond was 2.5 carats with four smaller diamonds around it and two down each shaft, all set in platinum.

Vera and Angus were having a rare night away from Claudette, Rory and the triplets. Mabel and Mrs Scribbins would be sleeping over at Iona House to keep Ivy company and together they would look after the children.

The bedrooms at Providence House would be full with Agatha and Charlie in Agatha's room, me in my room, the boys in their room and Vera and Angus in the guest room.

Ada looked radiant when I arrived at the party with John and Alfie. Her dress was pale yellow silk with pink peonies and trailing vines in the print. The skirt was full and mid-calf length which swished and swirled as she walked. Ian, looking extremely happy, made a handsome groom-to-be wearing his kilt and sporran with a crisp white shirt.

The barn looked lovely, set out with tables, chairs and some straw bales. I recognised some bunting which Ada had found, together with fairy lights in a cupboard at Hampton House. The walls and beams of the barn were now brightly lit and decorated, creating a fun, festive atmosphere befitting the celebration.

Hilda and I settled at a table with our plates of food, saving two seats for Agatha and Charlie.

"I've heard Frank has left the chemist shop in Burside," Hilda said.

"What, left for good?" I asked.

"As far as I know she has," Hilda answered, "devastated she was when 'he' was murdered. That's what Maureen who works there says."

Circlet of Gold

"I wonder where she's gone," I queried.

"Not sure exactly; seemingly she has an aunt abroad somewhere, New Zealand I think that's what Maureen said," explained Hilda.

"Goodness me, do you really think she would go to New Zealand, that's the other side of the world?" I queried.

"I'd put money on it. Couldn't face the fact that her mother murdered her fiancé," Hilda answered with conviction.

Agatha and Charlie joined us so the subject was quickly changed and we made a start on eating the delicious food.

"Have you heard about The Manor?" Hilda asked.

"No," I answered, "only that it is to be sold."

"Well, I've heard it has been sold," Hilda stated with the authority of one who knows.

"Yes, I heard that as well," said Agatha.

"I wonder who's bought it," I said, adding, "I imagine they'll be gentry."

"The marble goddess we bought at The Manor sale looks well by the pond at Providence House," Charlie said.

"It does that," said Agatha dreamily, "we've spent many an hour out there on warm summer nights, star gazing."

We ate our delicious supper of tender hog roast with jacket potatoes and all manner of salads.

The haunting sound of bagpipes could be heard outside the barn. Then, as the sound grew closer and louder a piper in full highland dress piped in the engagement cake. It was a magnificent cake, made and decorated by Mrs Davis which just goes to show she had no hard feelings about Ada dumping her son Emrys.

A feeling of excitement filled the room as Ian and Ada took to the floor to start the dancing. Once again I felt that sad *déjà vu* feeling overtaking me; I missed Adam and longed for him to be with me.

Vera and Angus were enjoying the dancing and although I felt lonely I understood that Adam was away doing important work for Nick so I would need to content myself with chatting to Hilda, Agatha and Charlie.

I looked up and for a moment I thought I was seeing things. Adam was walking towards me, Adam who was in Germany or was it London? No he was here at Rookery Farm. He spoke politely and briefly to my companions then led me by the hand onto the dance floor.

"You didn't think I'd miss Ada and Ian's engagement party did you?" he said, holding me close.

"How did you get here?" I asked.

"Special travel arrangements, laid on by Nick," he answered.

"How special?" was my next question.

"A racing driver and a two litre Alta sports car. I hope you don't mind but Duncan, he's the driver, is sleeping at the moment in the studio at Providence House," Adam explained.

"That's fine," I said, not quite believing that Adam was at the party.

I then asked, "How long are you staying?" dreading that the answer might be 'only a few hours'.

"I'm here until tomorrow then I'm going to visit my parents in Denstag then back to London. Oh and a bit of business in York on the way," he answered.

"You become more of a mystery the longer I know you," I said, thinking aloud. Then to myself I thought, 'don't complain, just make the most of him being here'.

The engagement party was a huge success and I danced with Adam until midnight. He squeezed into the back seat of my little Morris Minor with John and Alfie to allow Hilda to sit in the front seat which had more leg room.

Pip and Logan greeted us all very excitedly when we arrived back at Providence House, Little Laxlet.

"Where are you going to sleep?" Alfie asked Adam.

"Not sure," Adam replied, looking at me.

"Well Auntie Vera and Uncle Angus are in the guest room," said John.

"We used to sleep in the hayloft," said Alfie.

"I don't really think Adam wants to sleep in the hayloft," I quickly interjected.

"Oh I don't mind," said Adam.

"There's spiders and mice up there," said John.

"I know what," said Alfie, in a most commanding manner for a child so young "this might help to resolve the situation."

"What?" I said, wondering what his suggestion might be.

"It's obvious," said Alfie, "I'll go in Bettina's bed with her and you can have my bed."

"That is most kind of you Alfie," Adam said, giving me a resigned look.

Alfie cuddled into me which was cosy and lovely but I couldn't help thinking about my love life and wondering if it would ever get off the ground.

Following a massive family breakfast we said goodbye to Vera and Angus who needed to travel back to Iona House to be with the children.

Adam and I went for a walk with Pip and Logan. The boys had wanted to accompany us but I resorted to something I would not normally do. I offered them extra pocket money to stay at home; following some tricky negotiation, they found double pocket money for two weeks to be acceptable.

The village looked beautiful in its autumn colours as we walked hand in hand with the dogs who sniffed every gatepost.

Adam told me about his successful trip to Germany and how two printing presses would now be on their way to America.

"But what were you doing in London?" I asked.

"Oh, this and that. All to do with the new company Nick is setting up," he replied.

I had a feeling Adam was avoiding answering my question.

We were passing the telephone box on the green when he said, "Remember that, it's where we had our first kiss."

"Yes, of course I remember," I said.

"Let's go in for old times sake," he said, gently pulling me towards the telephone box.

Pip was unsure about the confined space but with some persuasion she joined us with Logan choosing to wait outside.

Adam slid his arms around my waist. I ran my hands up to his shoulders then around the back of his neck, feeling my fingers go deep into his soft brown hair. Our lips met, tender and light at first then quickly deepening into a crushing, wonderful kiss.

With my head resting on his chest he said, "I love you Bettina, when do you think we can be married?"

"I love you too Adam and I want us to be married more than anything in the whole world," I responded truthfully.

"Shall we set a date then?" he said.

"But what about living in America or rather, not living in America?" I asked.

"Don't worry about that. It's looking as though I'll be based in London now. I accept that you feel responsible for the boys so you stay in the north with them and we'll get together as often as we can," he explained, making it sound so simple.

We kissed again, a long, lingering, tender kiss.

"Ada and Ian are planning a May wedding," I then said.

"May 1937 seems a long way off," Adam responded.

"I know, but the weather should be nice for a wedding, our wedding," I said.

"May it is then," he said.

The kiss which followed was long and sensitive. A kiss which sealed our decision to be married in May.

Pip and Logan barked as old Joe Perkins tapped on the window and pointed to his pocket watch.

"Time to go," I said.

"Yes I must hit the road if I'm to see my parents then head off to York, then London, then America. Duncan should be out of bed by now and ready to leave. Agatha and Charlie said they would give him a good Yorkshire breakfast.

I did wonder what Adam's job really was. However I had made the decision not to ask. 'He'll tell me when he's ready,' I thought.

21

The Surprise

October 1936

"**She's got her** divorce, well the nisi, so I've heard," Mrs Handyside said over our morning cuppa.

"Ooooo ... now the fat'll be in the fire up at the palace," Mrs Scribbins added, then asked, "'ow do you know that Edna?"

"Well," Mrs Handyside said, "that housekeeper of Lady Dillmont-Preast, Mrs Proud I think her name was; well she called in a couple of days ago for that parcel Bettina had left for her Ladyship. We had a cup of tea together and that's how I know – decree nisi she said. Lady Dillmont-Preast knows Mrs Simpson and the King. In the same 'set' whatever that is, Mrs Proud told me."

"Didn't she say they'd all been to an 'ouseparty weekend at Leeds Castle," Mrs Scribbins added.

"Yes, and the funny thing is Leeds Castle is nowhere near Leeds. Even Mrs Proud was surprised at that," Mrs Handyside said.

"I think the King really is in love with her," I said, handing around the biscuits.

"That's as maybe, but twice divorced, she'll never be our queen," said Mrs Handyside, sucking in her breath, then adding, "never been much in the papers about them, keeping it very quiet."

"Do you suppose Queen Mary has met her?" I asked.

"Well *I've* heard she hasn't, won't have the likes of her up at the palace," said Mrs Handyside.

"True love. I reckon you knows it when it 'appens," sighed Mrs Scribbins.

I knew I loved Adam with all my heart but my love and responsibility for John and Alfie meant I couldn't go along with all of his plans for us.

"Where's your Adam just now?" Mrs Handyside asked.

"In America finishing his studies then he has a job in England for Nick Van der Linden," I replied.

"Job in England. I'd like to bet it's not 'round here," Mrs Handyside said.

"Not sure," I said, not wanting any further questions.

"My Stan and Phyllis will be tying the knot next year. Saving up they've been. Saving up for a house. Some new ones being built out near Mallard Hall, quite near Ian's place," Mrs Handyside said.

"Esther told me Hian's 'ouse is up for sale," Mrs Scribbins said.

"Up for sale. Now that is interesting," Mrs Handyside said, then added, "maybe me and Phyllis could go for a viewing. I've always fancied a look inside."

The telephone rang in the hall and I answered it to a tearful Ada; which was most unusual.

"What ever is wrong?" I asked.

She was sobbing loudly but managed to say between sobs, "Can't talk about it on the phone."

'This must be something serious' I thought, whilst asking, "Is there a problem with Ian?"

The sobbing became louder. "Is it Raven?" I asked.

Circlet of Gold

"No" she managed to say between sobs.

"Have you told Ian about whatever is worrying you?" I asked.

The sobs now turned into wailing.

"Where are you?" was my next question.

"Phone box on the green, Little Laxlet," she sniffed.

"Go to Providence House, Agatha is there, I'll see you in an hour or so," I instructed my distraught friend.

With Pip beside me I drove to Little Laxlet, the rain pounding so hard on the windscreen the wipers barely coped.

Ada seemed calmer when we met but insisted on going up to my bedroom to discuss the problem.

Agatha picked up several soaking wet handkerchiefs and gave Ada three clean, dry ones.

Once inside my bedroom and with the door shut, Ada's lips trembled, but no words came forth. Tears spouted from her red, swollen eyes and her face was now extremely blotchy from weeping.

Eventually she said, "Me dad is going to kill me."

"I doubt it," I said, wondering what on earth had happened.

"He'll kill me, I know he will," she kept repeating between her sobs.

"Come and sit on the bed and tell me what you've done," I said, patting the quilt.

"Only gone and got meself in the fucking club," she wailed, adding "He's very strict me dad, he'll never speak to me again."

'Oh well,' I thought, 'that's better than killing her.'

"It takes two you know, Ian needs to be told," I said in

what I hoped was a kind but firm tone.

This only caused Ada to prostrate herself on the bed and sob into the pillow.

I sat beside her on the bed feeling that a pause in the conversation was appropriate.

"What's it going to look like?" she said, sniffing now more than sobbing.

"Look like?" I asked, somewhat bemused.

"*Me*," she clarified, "walking up the aisle in May looking like a barrage balloon."

"That won't happen if you bring the wedding forward," was my practical suggestion.

"But it's all planned for May when the sun is shining and the blossoms are out," she said sadly.

"How far pregnant are you?" I asked.

"I've missed once. I was due on two weeks ago," she answered, no longer crying.

"So at this stage it's very early, are you sure?" I said.

"Course I'm sure, regular as clockwork me," she answered.

"Look at it like this," I said, to a now calmer Ada. "Think how beautiful a Christmas wedding would be. We can adapt the dress pattern and a huge bouquet will cover the bump, which shouldn't be very big by Christmas anyway."

There was a knock on the bedroom door, which I answered to Agatha, assuring her that everything was alright and thanking her for the two cups of tea and plate of cheese straws she had brought for us.

"It'll be bloody freezing in that church in December," Ada said.

"Well then, we'll just have to dress warmly," was my response.

Sitting on my bed propped up with pillows we sipped our tea and ate the delicious, crispy cheese straws.

"How about you tell Ian first, then I'm sure he'll go with you to tell your dad," I suggested.

"But it's not what I wanted," she said, starting to cry again.

"I know, I know," I said, "but we are where we are, and do you know what?"

"What?" she asked, large tears pouring down her cheeks.

"I reckon Ian will be thrilled to bits," I said, keeping my fingers crossed.

"What if he dumps me?" wailed Ada.

"Now why on earth would he dump you. He loves you and you love him," I said, feeling that I was now beginning to run out of consoling remarks.

There was another knock on the bedroom door.

I opened it to Agatha who said to me, "It's Ian on the phone asking for you."

I went downstairs to the telephone and said hello to Ian.

"Hello Bettina, I don't suppose you know where Ada is do you. I have a surprise for her," he said.

"She's here Ian," I said, thinking 'and boy does she have a surprise for you.'

"Are you two busy?" was his next question.

"No, just discussing the wedding dress," I answered, trying to sound convincing.

"That's fine," he said in an excited voice, then added, "please would you ask Ada to wait with you at Providence House and I will pick her up at 2pm.

"Will do, bye Ian," I said.

Back in the bedroom I said to Ada, "Ian is coming here for you at 2pm so go and splash your face with cold water.

This isn't a time for tears. He says he has a surprise for you."

Whilst Ada brushed her dark, lustrous wavy hair I looked for some make-up to hide her blotches. By the time Ian arrived she looked flushed and still a little puffy around the eyes, but more her usual, confident self.

As I helped Ada into her coat I said, "That brown skirt and mustard sweater really suit you. I don't know where you're going but you look lovely so have a nice time."

Buttoning her coat against the October north wind Ada then left Providence House to join Ian in the blue Riley Kestrel and await the disclosure of 'the surprise'.

Ian handed Ada an incredibly large key.

"What a large key," she said, thinking 'the door for this must be a big bugger.'

"It is," Ian said, smiling and giving Ada a loving glance.

"What's it for?" Ada asked.

"Just hold the key and close your eyes," Ian instructed.

They drove for a mile or so before the car stopped with a crunch on gravel.

"Open your eyes," Ian said.

"We're at The Manor," Ada said, then asked "Is there something on?"

"What is on my darling is that we are now going to look inside our new home," was his answer.

"But this is The Manor. I'm thunderstruck Ian. Our new home, are you sure?" Ada said, feeling confused.

"Try the key in the door," Ian said.

This she did and the massive oak door swung open onto an impressive hall with an equally impressive staircase.

"I haven't quite finalised the deal but the agent has given

us the key so we can have a look around," Ian said to a somewhat stunned Ada.

She then said, "Oh Ian, it's *The Manor*, it's amazing, are we really going to live here?"

"Yes we are, but only if you like it," he said, taking her hand. "Come on let's look around, the furniture you'll see in some of the rooms is what was left after the auction. I've negotiated that it stays with the house."

Ada and Ian walked from one fabulous room to another.

"That's a funny little room," Ada said.

Ian consulted the floor plan the agent had given him then said, "It's a butler's pantry."

"The kitchen is huge," Ada said, going over to the massive inglenook fireplace with iron rods for spit roasting.

"We'll need staff," Ian said.

"Staff?" Ada repeated, thinking 'hells bells, I've never had staff before'.

"Yes, one thought I've had is that my driver might reside in the flat above the garage. His wife has already expressed an interest in the post of housekeeper," said Ian.

"One thing," said Ada, looking out of the landing window at the rolling acres of land, "there'll be plenty of room for Raven and Eeyore."

"Do you think Edwin and Seth will like the house?" Ian asked.

"I don't see any reason why they wouldn't," replied Ada, whose thoughts were more along the lines of 'I'm getting used to this, I could do up the stables and have more horses, maybe even have a stud.'

"Which bedroom do you think we should have?" Ian asked as they began to look at the rooms on the first floor.

"This one is lovely, it looks over the deer park," said Ada, sitting on a double bed on which there was a mattress covered with a dust sheet.

"Do you like this bed or shall we replace it with the four poster we bought at the auction?" Ian asked.

"Mmm, just not sure. There's so much to take in," replied Ada, moving onto the bed and lying down.

Almost immediately Ian was lying beside her and as he slipped his hand under her mustard sweater he said, "I love you so much Ada and all I want is for us to be happy here."

Quickly and without hesitation they stripped each other naked on that cold October afternoon. The temperature in the bedroom was only 10 degrees Fahrenheit but so intense was the heat and passion they generated, neither of them even noticed.

He kissed her lips with ardour and desire which Ada returned in equal measure. As Ian entered her, she was warm, moist and welcoming. He knew in that moment that this beautiful, incredibly sexy woman was the person he wanted to spend the rest of his life with. There was no need for haste so together they enjoyed making love in what was to become their bedroom in their new home.

She shouted and moaned, as was her preferential mode of expression and together they experienced perfection.

Afterwards, sticking together they shared several warm loving post coital kisses. Declaring their love for each other once again and pulling the dust sheet around them; prior to falling into a deep sleep which lasted for about an hour.

"Darling Ian, I have something to tell you," Ada said into Ian's shoulder as she awoke.

Half dozing Ian said, "Mmm what's that."

"I think I'm pregnant, well I *know* I'm pregnant," she said, coming straight to the point.

"Pregnant," Ian murmured.

"Yes, pregnant as in having a baby," said Ada who was now starting to feel worried.

"Hardly surprising I suppose, we make love at every opportunity we can," he said.

"You're not angry then," she said, feeling more relieved.

"Angry, no, why should I be angry. This baby is made with love," he said, stroking her waist, pubic hair and thighs.

"We might need to bring the wedding forward to – say Christmas," Ada tentatively said.

"Christmas sounds wonderful," he said, starting to kiss her nipples.

"Ian," Ada said, raising herself onto one elbow then kissing him gently on the lips.

"Yes my darling Ada, what is worrying you and why are you frowning?" he said.

"Will you do me a favour?" she said.

"If I can," he responded, now fondling her breasts.

"Will you tell me dad for me?"

The answer was in his loving kiss, foreplay and further love making.

Ada's thoughts momentarily were, 'Ian'll tell me dad, thank God for that'.

22

Love

"**What are you** doing for your twenty first. It's this month isn't it?" Mrs Scribbins asked as we drove to the Morgan for our volunteering with the library trolley.

"Nothing planned," I replied, "with Adam away I don't feel like a party."

"Shame that. You must really love 'im," she sighed.

"I do," I said.

"Me and my Wallace we was in love, truly in love. Married in 1913," Mrs Scribbins said.

"Do you know what Mrs Scribbins I don't think I've ever heard you mention your husband before," I said.

"No, well I've been a widda woman a long time now," she said.

"Where did you meet. Was he a soldier?" I asked, curiously.

"Not when I met 'im 'e wasn't. We met on the railway line," was her reply.

Assuming I'd misheard I said, "Was that on a train or in the station?"

"No, it's as I said. We met on the track," she said.

"Tell me about it, I'm intrigued," I requested.

"Well when I was a girl I 'ad a nice little job at Ransington railway station," she said, adding, "me job it were in catering."

"Catering. As in cafe or restaurant?" I stupidly asked.

"No, as in trolley," she replied.

"Trolley?" I repeated.

" Yes, trolley. Massive it were, steel with an hurn. Me job was to fill the hurn with water and set it to boil. While it was coming to the boil I'd make me sandwiches and fill up the trolley. 'Am was me best seller. Cakes, plenty of cakes, not made by me though. Then hide load up with cups, saucers, plates and spoons. A big jug of milk and a bowl of sugar," she said.

"Sounds quite a load," was my comment.

"Certainly was Bettina. Very 'eavy and 'ard to push," she said with feeling.

"I can imagine," I said.

"Well I was only a slip of a girl at the time and the stuck wheels made it even 'arder to push," she said.

"What was it you had to do with your loaded trolley?" I asked.

"Served the passengers on the long distance I did. That's the trains what go from London to Scotland and Scotland to London. Always stopped at Ransington for 'arf an hour," she explained.

"Did they get off the train to buy the refreshments, the passengers?" I asked.

"Oh no. I walked, pushin me trolley and they bought tea and sandwiches through the open winders," she said.

"That sounds like hard work, pushing a heavy trolley the full length of a long train," I said.

"It was. Then I 'ad to push it back again to gather in the pots afore I washed 'em," she said.

"There must have been a problem with the trolley. The library trolley is easy to manoeuvre," I said.

"Problem. I'll say there was a problem. The problem was

muck. The wheels was full o muck," she said with feeling, then added, "to get hit onto the platform I 'ad to give it a right 'efty push."

"You must have been quite strong," I said.

"Allus 'ad strong harms," she said, then continued, "One day Mr Bell, 'e was the Stationmaster, 'e says to me as I started me early shift at six o'clock in the morning, 'e says 'we've got a new porter starting today Maud. A young man by the name of Scribbins, Wallace Scribbins.'

"Well I didn't take a lot of notice," she went on, "just busied meself makin the sandwiches and loading up me trolley. At half past seven Mr Bell says, looking at 'is watch, 'better get out there Maud, the 7:42 will be here in twelve minutes.'

"Righty e ho! I said, givin me trolley hits usual 'efty shove out of the kitchen.

Like at the pictures it were. Me trolley fair flew across the platform, tipped over the edge and landed on the line. I couldn't stop it. Well you can imagine the commotion. The 7:42 luckily was running five minutes late and it had to be stopped about a mile outside Ransington station. Mr Bell runnin around wavin 'is red flag and blowin 'is whistle. 'Keep back, keep back 'e shouted to the passengers waiting to catch the train.

Hit was fortunate that one of the porters 'ad the common sense to send a message up the line to the signal box."

"Quite a commotion," I agreed.

"All me lovely sandwiches gone to waste and the pots all smashed. I climbed down onto the track and through me tears I saw this lovely young man, 'andsome 'e was and 'e were down on the track as well. Jumped down 'e 'ad. 'Don't worry' 'e said. Very calm 'e was. 'Come on I'll give you an 'and' and together we cleared up the mess.

There were a few soldiers waiting for the train and they 'elped lift the trolley and the hurn back up onto the platform.

A bit later when things had calmed down Mr Bell said, 'I thought you'd notice I'd cleaned out the trolley wheels for you Maud'. I said 'I didn't Mr Bell or I wouldn't 'av given hit such an efty push.'

Mr Bell then said, 'by the way Maud this is Wallace Scribbins our new porter. I looked into 'is eyes, Wallace that is not Mr Bell, and do you know what Bettina?"

"What," I said.

"It were love at first sight. Love at first sight it were for the both of us," she said, dreamily.

"That is so romantic," I said.

"Oh it was. We 'ad a nice little flat. Then Mabel came along. But then my darling Wally 'ad to go to war and that was it. 'E never came back. 'Is name is on the Cenotaph though," she said.

We had arrived at the Morgan and I needed to dab my eyes with my handkerchief.

"Thank you for telling me your story Mrs Scribbins. I didn't know your name was Maud until today," I said.

"Yes but me friends call me Maudy. You can call me Maudy if you like," she said.

"Come on then Maudy, let's go and push the library trolley and I promise not to give it one of those hefty pushes you are famous for.

23

A Golden Crown

By 10am every morning I was at Providence House, Little Laxlet, designing and making, with Agatha, underwear for 'Lingerie Chic'. Enquiries poured in, especially for our cami-knickers, for which we received many complimentary letters of thanks. We no longer needed to advertise as our order book was full and there was a waiting list for our garments, mostly from titled aristocracy.

Today, November 29th, 1936 was a special day as Ada was coming over for a fitting of her wedding dress.

"My tummy's flat-ish now," she said, "but do you think I'll be showing in a month?"

"I've cut the dress generously, just in case you are," I assured her, "but you hardly show at all at the moment. Anyway we can make adjustments even at the last minute if we have to."

The dress, made from white satin, was a simple design with a high neckline. Tiny, satin covered buttons placed centre front from neck to waist then continuing down the skirt to the hem.. The long sleeves with puff shoulders, which were the height of fashion that year, went to points onto the hands. The skirt of the dress was long and draped into a train at the back.

"I'll be wearing a fur coat to go to the church," Ada said. "It's me mam's, she's never worn it."

Circlet of Gold

"Has your dad come 'round?" I asked.

"I think so, but he hasn't got over the shock of us wanting a Christmas wedding," she replied.

"Tell us again" Agatha and I both requested. "Tell us again what he said."

Ada then impersonated her dad.

"Christmas wedding! Christmas wedding! I'll be buggered if you'll be having a Christmas wedding. What with me up to me oxters in turkeys and your mother'll be plucking from morning 'till night."

Agatha and I, for some reason, found this very funny and were both creased with laughter.

"Then what did he say," we both asked, bearing in mind that Mr Smith's future son in law was a judge.

Ada then again impersonated her dad.

"Christmas wedding! Christmas wedding! It's our busiest time of year and you two have t' cheek to want a Christmas wedding. How in hells name doest tha think I'll have time to take mother off her plucking and walk you up t' aisle."

By this time all three of us were in fits of laughter.

The wedding date was now set to be Tuesday December 29th, 1936 and Ada had been quite relieved that her dad had taken the idea of her early marriage so well.

I was to be bridesmaid and Delicia matron of honour. Ada's sister Molly would also have been matron of honour as well but she was now seven months pregnant.

"Are you absolutely sure you want Delicia and me to wear white?" I asked.

"Oh yes, one hundred percent sure, with royal blue velvet capes," she replied.

"Royal blue velvet capes!" I exclaimed as this was the first mention of capes. I was stunned as each time I saw Ada she added extras.

"Has Delicia sent you her measurements?" Ada asked, oblivious to my shocked response regarding the blue velvet capes.

"Yes," I answered, "she is a similar size to me, only a bit taller, I can have her dress ready for her to try on when she comes to aunt Eliza Jane's for Christmas."

"I just loved the veil she wore at her wedding," Ada said, dreamily.

"It is beautiful," I said, "it's Carrickmacross lace. Would you like me to ask aunt Eliza Jane if you can wear it for your wedding?"

"Oh yes please, then Delicia can bring it with her and it will be my something borrowed," Ada replied.

"Have you thought about a headdress to go with the veil?" I asked.

"A crown, a golden crown," she said decisively, adding, "but I haven't got one."

"Sounds perfect," I said, thinking 'Where in the world will I find a golden crown so close to the wedding?'

"Flowers. Have you decided on flowers?" I asked, knowing that Mr Handyside always had a good selection of spring flowers blooming early in his heated greenhouse. Phyllis, who had left her job at the department store and now ran her own florestry business, would be making the bouquets.

"Orchids would be nice and lily of the valley," Ada answered.

"Let's try on your dress," I said, thinking, 'orchids not a problem as orchids were Mr Handyside's speciality. Lily of the valley might need a miracle.'

"Me tits have grown huge," said Ada, rearranging her bust as she stepped into the white satin dress.

"Good job I've cut your dress on the generous side then," I said, fastening the tiny satin buttons.

Turning to the full length mirror she purred, "Oh it's gorgeous Bettina. I look, well I look, nigh on virginal."

Agatha and I both commented on how lovely Ada looked.

As I pinned and adjusted the wedding dress I couldn't help wishing it was mine and that I would be marrying Adam on December 29th.

"Mrs Davis will be catering for over a hundred guests, and the purchase of The Manor is complete so we will be having the reception there, in the ballroom," Ada said decisively.

"That's a huge number to cater for," I said.

"I know, but the girl who's taken over the tenancy for Groat Cottage is a cook up at the camp and they're doing it together," she said.

"Still, a hundred, it's a lot of work for two," Agatha said.

"Now don't worry yourselves. A couple of my old boyfriends are in the catering corps of the Engineers Regiment up at the camp. Their senior officer, Major Oldroyd, who by the way will be a guest with his wife at the wedding, is a friend of Ian's so no probs. Stop worrying," she said, "those lads'll have that old kitchen up at The Manor singing and dancing to their tune in no time. Used to numbers they are."

"All sounds very organised," I said, thinking, 'old boyfriends have their uses.'

"Our Sammy, me brother in law, well he'll be in charge of the drink. Gone right off it meself," Ada said, stepping out of her bridal gown.

"Sounds like it's going to be a grand party," Agatha said.

"It will that," affirmed Ada, "I hope your Charlie will be coming up for the wedding?"

"She is. Do you want me to telephone and see if Hadleigh's Mill have any royal blue silk velvet and silk lining?" said Agatha.

"Yes please Agatha. Did I tell you Ian's arranged a surprise honeymoon?" Ada said excitedly.

"No, where?" I said as we moved into the kitchen for our cuppa.

"I've no idea. I suppose it wouldn't be a surprise if he told me. He's full of surprises and they're all fantastic," Ada said.

"What do Seth and Edwin think about having a new baby brother or sister?" I asked, adding, "it must have been quite a surprise for them."

"Well I must say I was a bit concerned about that, but do you know what, they love the idea. They're going to ush at the wedding," she said.

"Ush?" I repeated.

"Yes ush. You know ushing. Giving out the order of service and showing people to their seats," Ada confirmed.

"The church will be packed," said Agatha, who had returned from placing the order with Hadleigh's Mill.

"I know," said Ada. "Just as well, it'll be the only way to keep fucking warm."

When I arrived back at Iona House that afternoon there was a letter waiting for me. I recognised Adam's handwriting.

2309 21ˢᵗ Street,
Queens,
New York.

23ʳᵈ November, 1936.

My Darling Bettina,

I'm sorry I was not home for your birthday and this letter is to say it's unlikely I'll be home for Christmas. However I do have Ada and Ian's wedding date in my diary and will definitely be home for that.
I just wish it was us getting married on the 29ᵗʰ December but I suppose May will soon be here.
In the meantime you and I are going on a holiday – John and Alfie too. Please apply for passports for all three of you without delay then leave the rest to me.
I love you and am longing to see you again.

Love,

Adam xxxx

Passports, a holiday in a foreign country for me and the boys. I felt quite perplexed. Adam often went to France and Germany with his work – how I hoped the holiday wouldn't be in Germany with all the problems there were in 1936.

There would be a form to complete for me and one for each of the boys; as their legal guardian I would get on to it first thing in the morning.

I'd been so busy with making underwear and now Ada's wedding dress plus bridesmaids dresses for Delicia and me, I had not even touched the blue and white fabric I'd bought to make a nine patch quilt. 'Life just gets in the way' I thought. Not to worry, I told myself, once Ada and Ian's wedding is over and I'm on holiday I can relax and perhaps focus on my quilting.

December 11th, 1936

"You look a tad shattered," Vera said, as we washed and dried the dishes after dinner at Iona House.

"I am, you're right. I'm in need of this holiday Adam's arranging for us," I said.

"Where are you going?" Vera asked.

"Don't know and don't much care, it will be fabulous just to be on holiday," I replied.

"Would you like to join Angus and me this evening once the children are all in bed?" she said.

"That would be lovely," I replied, adding "but don't be too shocked if I nod off."

Consulting the Radio Times, Vera said, "The Comic Opera is on the wireless at 9:40pm, do you fancy that?"

"Sounds good," I said, "will we be having cocoa, the way we used to in the old days?" I said.

"Yes", she said, laughing, "who would ever have thought we'd have seven children living in Iona House."

We were enjoying the music when it was suddenly interrupted by a serious male voice which said:-

"This is Windsor Castle. His Royal Highness, Prince Edward."

We sat there in silence listening to Prince Edward, who until the previous day had been our King, telling the nation that he had abdicated the throne to marry the woman he loved, Wallace Simpson.

His younger brother was now our King; he then swore allegiance to him.

"Well," said Angus, "a constitutional crisis has been avoided, I expect he will leave the country within hours."

Vera said, "I'd heard he was besotted with love for her but I never thought he would go this far."

"Do you think they will come back when they are married?" I said.

"Doubt that very much," said Angus.

24

The Carol Service

The short, dark days of December were flying over. Agatha and I were busy packing the Christmas orders for 'Lingerie Chic'. My spare time was spent working on finishing the two bridesmaids dresses and velvet capes. Ada's wedding dress was completed, hanging on the tailors dummy and covered with a sheet.

I had written to great aunt Eliza Jane and asked if Ada could use the Carrickmacross lace veil for her wedding and my aunt had agreed and confirmed that Delicia would bring it with her. The headdress of a golden crown, requested by Ada, continued to enter my thoughts and I concluded that she may just have to settle for the wax orange blossom and tulle flowered headdress Phyllis had constructed.

I rarely had a minute to think about the holiday but had begun to feel concerned that our passports had not arrived.

By December 17th I'd heard nothing and Vera suggested asking Ian to see if he could hurry things along. Bearing in mind the fact that he was a judge I contacted him and he said he would look into it for me.

This worked and on December 20th 1936 our passports arrived. That's one thing less to worry about, I thought, putting them into my document holder with our birth certificates which I always kept in the drawer of mam's treadle sewing machine.

Mrs Scribbins and I took the library trolley around the wards of the Morgan Endowment Hospital on Wednesday December 23rd. I really felt I did not have the time, but this was the last visit until after the holidays and Maudy particularly wanted to go as she'd heard there was to be a carol service.

A young woman of about my age was looking at the books with a view to borrowing one when I realised I knew her.

"Hello," I said. "It's Verity Vinadine isn't it? You're a long way from home."

"Hello Bettina," she replied. "I am that and they're wanting me to stay in 'till after t' New Year."

"Oh. I hope it's not serious," I said, feeling concerned for her health.

"No, it's nowt really. I came in a few days ago. Dr Blackwood thought I wasn't eating properly and it's lonely up at the farm since mother passed last year."

"Who's looking after the farm for you?" I asked.

"I've only got a few sheep now and one beast. Jock Latimer from t' next farm has taken 'em ower to his place, along wi' me dog Bess. The house 'll be all right though, nobody goes up there much," she said.

"It seems a shame to have to stay in hospital all the same," I said, thinking she may have a relative she could stay with.

"Gets awful lonesome int' winter out on the fell. Not so bad int' summer. They're very kind here, the nurses," Verity said, choosing 'Ann of Green Gables' to read.

We then heard the distant voices of carol singers.

As the choir approached our ward the sound became louder; they entered singing 'In The Bleak Mid Winter'. Nurses, wearing their cloaks inside out to show the red lining, all grouped around the Christmas tree. They carried lanterns and the main lights were dimmed.

Maudy and I each took a seat beside a bed and listened to the pure voices of these young women; most of whom had already worked either a day or night shift but still found time to sing so sweetly for their patients.

They sang three carols then left; their rubber soled shoes making no noise. Only the rustle of their starched aprons accompanied 'It Came Upon A Midnight Clear'.

Looking around I noticed a few tears being shed by the patients.

Verity, now back in her bed, dabbed her eyes and said, "Wasn't that lovely?"

"It certainly was," I agreed.

"It's the company I miss. I've really enjoyed my few days here but there's nowt wrong with me, not really," Verity said.

"How do you pass the time?" I asked, thinking I could bring her a jig-saw puzzle or some embroidery.

"Well I read and give the nurses a helping hand," she replied.

"They must be glad of your help," I said, then asked, "what is it you do for them?"

"Oh I'm a dab hand at it now. I help make cotton wool balls and fold gauze dressings to fill those big steel drums for autoclaving," she replied.

"I'm sure the nurses are very appreciative," I said.

"I heard Ada Smith were getting wed," Verity said.

"That's right, she is. I've made her wedding dress," I said.

"I didn't know you could sew Bettina Dawson. I knew your mam could. You must have inherited it," Verity said.

"You might say that," I said, "my aunt Agatha and I have a little business in Little Laxlet making underwear."

"I've never been to a wedding," Verity said with a sad tone in her voice.

"Never" I said.

"No. We kept ourselves to ourselves up at farm. There's only me now and I don't have any cousins," she said, adding with a sigh, "Oh it must be lovely to go to a wedding."

Mrs Scribbins had taken the library trolley to the store cupboard and unloaded it and was now waiting for me at the entrance to the ward.

I said goodbye to Verity and wished her a Happy Christmas along with the nurses who were now bringing around the evening cocoa, Horlicks and Ovaltine.

"She seems a nice girl," Mrs Scribbins said, once we were in the car and obviously wanting to know more.

"She is. She's *very* nice; I know her from my school days," I said, adding, "she lives out on the fell, a lonely spot miles from anywhere. Gets snowed in most winters."

"What's she doin in the 'ospital?" Mrs Scribbins asked.

"In need of companionship mainly. Verity is lonely and not eating properly since her mother died last year. Her family doctor sent her in," I replied.

"Is she gonna be in over the Christmas and New Year?" Maud asked.

"Think so," I replied.

"Seems a shame it does with nothing wrong with 'er. The others in the ward looked a bit old, more your geriatrics, and 'er just a young girl," Maud said.

"It does and I know what you're thinking Maud Scribbins

and the answer is no, a definite no. I'm up to my eyes with preparations for Ada's wedding and tomorrow Delicia is coming for a fitting. It's a no," I replied in what was almost a rant.

"Just sayin. Seems a shame," she said sniffing, then stayed silent for the remainder of the journey back to her flat.

"Goodbye and Merry Christmas Maudy," I said as she was getting out of the car.

"Merry Christmas Bettina. I might see you up at The Manor afor the wedding. Me and Esther are going hover there to make up the beds for the visitors. Expect we'll give the rooms a bit of a dust as well," Mrs Scribbins said, adding "Stanley Handyside is taking us over there. I expects his mother will come as well."

"Doubt I'll be going over there before the wedding Maudy. Have a good Christmas." I said.

The next morning, following a telephone call to Matron, I collected Verity from the Morgan. John, Alfie and Pip were in the car with me and we motored on frosty roads to Little Laxlet where Agatha, Charlie and Logan would be waiting.

Due to Ada and Ian's wedding being the following Tuesday we would be spending Christmas at Providence House.

On arrival we were welcomed into the warm kitchen with the customary cup of tea and home made biscuits.

Although Agatha had not met Verity before she thought she had met her mother.

"Didn't your mam have a stall at Burside market?" Agatha asked.

"She did that. Eggs and sheep's cheese mostly," Verity answered.

"Yes I remember Mrs Vinadine now. I'm sorry she has passed," Agatha said, adding, "you live in a right out of the way spot Verity."

"I know and it's lonely since I left school and mam died," Verity said.

"Does Jock Latimer still have the next farm to you?" Agatha asked.

"Aye 'e does. 'E's looking after me stock for me," Verity said.

"How do you go on for food and the like?" Charlie asked.

"Well I grow a few veg. and Jock leaves bread n groceries in the nook int wall down t' track," she said.

"Mmm," said Agatha. Whom I knew was thinking, 'no wonder she looks so thin'.

"We're having turkey tomorrow," said Charlie, "I've been up to Rookery Farm for it this morning early."

"How are things up there?" I asked.

"Well Mr Smith and Ada had already left for Ransington market and, well you know Mrs Smith, alus calm. Mind that's a big goitre she's got in her neck," Charlie said.

"What time do you think Delicia will be here for her dress fitting?" Agatha asked.

"She said about one o'clock but it'll depend on the roads, there's already a dusting of snow," I replied.

At 1:15pm there was a knock at the front door and I opened it to Delicia, Ralph and Jude who ran straight into my arms.

He was now two years old and chattering away, curious about everything and I observed there was no longer any sign of his birthmark.

Circlet of Gold

Delicia and I had so much catching up to do, which we did, in the sewing room.

"Oh it's so lovely to see you again," she said.

"I couldn't agree more," I responded, then asked, "how are things in Scotland?"

"Okay, fine really, but the castle is so out of the way and Ralph is working full time, he is so busy with the estate," she said.

"What about his brother Quentin, doesn't he help?" I asked.

"Not at all," she said with feeling, "spends most of his time in London and now he's taking flying lessons."

"Does he still have the glamorous girlfriend?" I asked, remembering the stunning model from Delicia and Ralph's wedding.

"Yes, and Arjana likes London, that's the trouble," Delicia said.

"Jude looks fabulous," I said, adding, "he seems to be advanced for his age, a clever boy."

"He is, but you do realise that you are slightly biased," she said laughing.

There was a knock on the sewing room door and then Agatha popped her head in and asked, "I've shown Verity the guest room and now she's asking if she can come into the sewing room to see how we work."

Delicia, who was now standing in her underwear, said this would be fine and Verity and Agatha entered the room.

I suggested that Verity might hold the pin cushion and together we adjusted the hem of Delicia's bridesmaids dress.

"Your turn now," Delicia said.

I stripped to my underwear and slipped into my

bridesmaids dress. Agatha took over the pinning and once again Verity held the pin cushion.

"These must be the royal blue velvet capes you wrote about Bettina, they are sumptuous," said Delicia, stroking the velvet.

"I reckon we'll need them, it's freezing," I said.

Verity, who had not spoken a word since coming into the sewing room then said in a foreboding tone, "The weather is closing in."

"Closing in?" the three of us questioned.

"Oh aye, could be snowed in by tomorrow," she added.

Normally I would not have been concerned but with a wedding in five days time and a holiday shortly afterwards I, momentarily, felt apprehensive.

"Where are you staying for the wedding?" I asked Delicia.

"We're staying at The Manor. There will be a good few of us. Aunt Eliza Jane with Winnie, Gladys and their husbands, Vera, Angus and the five children, plus Mabel and Ivy to look after them. Of course Ian and his boys. I believe there will be other guests too. All arriving on the 28th.

"Have you seen The Manor yet?" I asked.

"No but I gather it's a fine property," Delicia answered.

"It's fabulous, mostly Jacobean but some of it dates back to Medieval times. The reception is to be in the ballroom," I said.

"Well, if we get snowed in there I doubt anyone would mind," Delicia said.

Verity said, "Me mam used to work up at The Manor, years ago, before Sir Simeon Styles bought it."

"Well, I didn't know *that!*" exclaimed Agatha who considered herself to knowledgeable about everything concerning Little Laxlet. She then added, "I seem to remember it belonged to a General something or other, now what on earth was his name? All the kids in the village were scared of him. Ooo ... it's on the tip of my tongue."

"Yes it was General Glendenning, it were him had the massive stables built, died in the Great War so mam left and married me dad," Verity said.

"Was he killed in the fighting?" Agatha asked.

"No," said Verity. "Silly old bugger managed to fall off the banister rail of the grand staircase; sliding down it 'e was, drunk as a lord – did for 'im."

She then added, "me mam liked a drink and she would tell me tales of The Manor and the goings on up there when she'd had a couple."

Charlie came into the sewing room to say she'd made a pot of tea and Jude wanted to see auntie Bettina.

More tales of the silly old bugger of a General would have to wait for another day.

25

Three

Christmas 1936 passed in a blur of royal blue velvet and stitching. Charlie, helped by Verity, cooked the dinner on Christmas day and it was delicious. Ada would be calling on Sunday 27th for her final dress fitting following which she would go over to see Mrs Davis to discuss food for the reception.

Providence House, although rather untidy, looked and smelled wonderful. We had a Christmas tree in the orangery, which the boys had decorated, and all manner of delicious treats emerged from the Aga.

Logan was in trouble. On Christmas morning Charlie had boiled the turkey giblets with an onion in readiness to make gravy with the stock. Due to a shortage of time, the enamel bowl containing the giblets and stock was covered with a plate and placed on the outside boot-room windowsill to cool. Of course Logan knocked the bowl down and enjoyed eating the contents, aided and abetted by Pip. Luckily we had some Bisto which, mixed with the turkey drippings, made excellent gravy.

At 10am on the 27th Ada arrived with her dad in his van which was full of chickens and turkeys dressed for the oven and several trays of eggs.

"Me dad's just running up to The Manor with stuff for the reception," said Ada as she came into the kitchen.

"How are you feeling?" I asked, thinking she looked rather peeky.

"Bit pukey if truth be told, threw up me breakfast this morning," she replied.

Verity said, "me mam recommends ginger tea for a bilious stomach."

"Eee Verity Vinadene fancy seeing you here, I haven't seen you in years!" exclaimed Ada.

"It's a long story Ada, but Verity is staying with us for a while. It's lonely up on the fell," I said, pouring hot water into a mug which contained a piece of crystallised ginger and putting some bread on the Aga to toast.

We sat in the warm kitchen and Ada drank her ginger tea, ate her toast with honey and began to look a little less pale; we then went through to the sewing room for her to try on her wedding dress.

"Have you brought your wedding shoes?" I asked.

"Yes" she said, delving in her bag and pulling out a shoe box containing white satin shoes with a kitten heel, which she then put on before trying on her wedding dress.

I made the necessary adjustments, which were only minor.

"I have a surprise for you, close your eyes," I said.

She did and when she opened them she saw I was holding the Carrickmacross lace wedding veil to which I had stitched the headdress of wax orange blossom and tulle flowers.

Ada was delighted to see the veil but I sensed her disappointment with the wax orange blossom and tulle.

When I placed the headdress on Ada's head and adjusted the veil I thought she made the most beautiful bride I'd ever seen. Her dark, lustrous hair framed her face which now had more colour and her smile was of pure happiness.

"May I bring the girls in to see you in your finery?" I asked.

"Yes, and if I say so meself Bettina Dawson you've made a grand job. I look good enough to marry a judge!"

Agatha, Charlie and Verity came into the sewing room and gave a round of applause, all exclaiming how wonderful Ada looked.

"What time is the wedding?" Verity asked.

"One o'clock Tuesday at St Luke's," Ada said, then added wistfully, "the headdress Phyllis has made is beautiful but I'd set me heart on a crown."

"Will it be all right if I come to t' church to see thee wed. I've never been to a wedding afore?" Verity asked.

"Course you can," answered Ada.

"What about the flowers?" said Charlie, "not the best time of year."

"Don't worry, it's all organised. Mr Handyside is growing something special for the wedding and Stan and Phyllis are bringing them over on Tuesday morning," I said.

"What about the button holes and corsages?" asked Agatha.

"Now stop worrying girls, it's all arranged," I said. "Stan is dropping Ada's bouquet, the bridesmaids' bouquets and some button holes and corsages off at Rookery Farm on the morning of the wedding, then the rest he's taking up to The Manor. See, all sorted," I said firmly whilst carefully removing the headdress and veil.

"You and Delicia will come over to me good and early, I might need calming down," Ada said, then added, "Did I tell you Ian's arranged a Rolls Royce for the church. First it'll take you, Delicia and me mam then come back for me and dad.

How posh is that?"

"Delicia is coming here, we'll change then drive over to you in plenty of time to leave for the church. John, Alfie and Hilda are going with Agatha and Charlie," I said in what I hoped was a reassuring voice.

"What about your dresses and capes?" Ada asked anxiously, stepping out of her wedding dress.

"All done, stop worrying," I said, adding "the capes have a pocket for a hanky and mine has an extra large pocket for additional items."

Charlie now owned an Austin seven which she kept in the garage at Providence House when she was staying. The garage had been converted from the tack room and apple store. She said, "Agatha and I will pick Hilda up and bring Verity as well as the boys."

"Stop worrying," we all said.

"Okay then I will stop worrying. Everything seems organised. I'll just pop over and see Mrs Davis about the catering," Ada said, adding almost as an affirmation "nothing is going to go wrong."

"Good. Stay positive," I said, giving her a hug.

"I will and I'll call back for me dress in about an hour," said Ada.

"Okay, it'll be ready," I said.

Ada called back for her wedding dress which was ready and packed in a dress bag with the Carrickmacross veil and headdress in a box.

Mr Smith, waiting in his van outside the house for Ada, tooted to let her know he was there.

I opened the door and as Ada was about to leave she said,

"Do you know what would be nice?"

"What?" I asked with trepidation and hoping she wouldn't mention the gold crown.

"Well, you know I've always wanted three bridesmaids, and our Molly is eight months gone now," she said.

"Mmmm," I murmured, holding my breath.

"Do you think you could run up another bridesmaids dress then Verity could be one as well?" Ada said.

"Just like that!" I exclaimed, astounded.

"I bet you can," she said, as she dashed out of the door, down the path and into the van.

The word miracle once again sprang to mind as I telephoned Stan to enquire about the flowers and tell him there would now be three bridesmaids.

Verity was delighted beyond delight at the thought of being a bridesmaid. However I made it clear that if she wanted a bridesmaids dress and cape in less than two days then she would be responsible for walking Pip and Logan as well as helping Charlie with the cooking. I knew that if I started straight away I could, with Agatha's help, make a dress and cape for her before the wedding.

"All hands to the pump it is then," Agatha said.

"Too right," I said, pinning the bridesmaids dress pattern to the white silk.

"She seems a sweet girl," Agatha said, pinning the cape pattern to the royal blue velvet.

"She is, I just wish she'd stop saying, 'the weather's closing in' I said.

"Good job we've got the garage cleared out. I'll get Charlie to put the cars inside tonight," was Agatha's response.

26

The Hiding Place

By mid afternoon that same Sunday Agatha and I were making good progress with the third bridesmaids dress and velvet cape when Verity and Charlie came into the sewing room with cups of tea and Christmas cake for us all.

"That looks really lovely," said Verity.

"It does that," said Charlie, handing the tea around the table.

"Almost ready for you to try on Verity," I said, "but I think Agatha and I will take a short break and enjoy our cuppa."

"I know where there's a crown," said Verity.

"Aye in the Tower of London," said Agatha.

"Yes but that's the Crown Jewels. This is a crown, a proper crown, but just a crown ... not royal or anything," Verity said.

"A real crown. Where?" I asked, not expecting an answer which might make sense.

"Up at The Manor," answered Verity.

"Up at The Manor," I repeated.

Verity had our full attention.

"Me mam told me about it. Gold it is and old, hundreds of years old. The old General, General Glendenning used to show it to her. Liked her to dress up for 'im. Called her 'is Princess. She told me she would wear it for special occasions," Verity said.

"What special occasions?" Charlie asked.

"Coronations. They often had a Coronation. She would crown him King then he would crown her Queen. They had outfits just for that," Verity said.

"He's been dead for years," I said, thinking 'this conversation is becoming fanciful and I still have a great deal of sewing to do'.

"I doubt it'll still be there" said Agatha. "after all Sir Simeon and Lady Rachael lived at The Manor for the best part of twenty years. It'll be gone now."

"Oh no. It's hidden," Verity said.

"Do you know where it is hidden?" I asked.

"Yes," Verity replied, adding, "but I'm sworn to secrecy."

"By whom? Who swore you to secrecy?" Charlie asked.

"Mam. Me mam swore me to secrecy," Verity said.

"Well," said Charlie, a smattering of frustration starting to appear in her voice, "I'm sure your mam would be delighted that you are going to be Ada's bridesmaid and she would want Ada to have the crown for her wedding. So tell us where it is hidden."

"Okay then," Verity calmly said, "it's in the priest-hole."

"Do you know where the priest-hole is?" asked Agatha.

"In a chimney, that's all I know, in a chimney," Verity replied.

I telephoned Ian and, without giving an exact reason why, asked if I could visit The Manor.

"Yes that will be fine Bettina," Ian said, "I'm going there myself later this afternoon, Mrs Davis is there already and Esther and Mrs Scribbins are preparing the guest rooms"

Charlie, Verity, John and Alfie squeezed in to my little Morris Minor and we drove up to The Manor. Agatha continued sewing with Pip and Logan keeping her company.

Mrs Davis was in the huge Manor kitchen with some of the soldiers from the camp starting the preparation for the wedding feast.

I hoped the search for the priest-hole would not take too long as I needed to finish Verity's bridesmaid's dress.

"Hello there," one of the soldiers said.

I recognised him from the dance in the officers mess, he'd been selling tickets on the door.

"Hello Max," I said, "we are here on an investigation."

"Sounds interesting," he replied.

"Could be if we find what we are looking for," I said.

"What are you looking for?"

"A priest-hole," I answered, adding "and we haven't got long."

"Strange thing to be looking for but just shout if you need a hand," he said, laughing.

We didn't quite know where to start as each room had a large fireplace as did every bedroom.

I had read somewhere that often a priest-hole would be adjacent to the bedroom of the mistress of the house which made giving food to the hidden priest less likely to be discovered.

The three larger bedrooms revealed nothing and Alfie and John were now becoming streaked with soot.

"LOOK IN HERE," shouted Charlie.

We all dashed to the bedroom where she was.

"This might be a possible," she said, "the tiles are loose in the hearth."

We lifted the loose tiles but the hearth was equally as solid as all the others.

Bedroom after bedroom we checked the fireplaces and

all seemed solid as all the others with no extra cavities in the chimney.

"I seem to recall mam mentioning a cupboard with a false back to it," said Verity.

'Why didn't she say that before?' I thought, but said, "In any particular room?"

"Where they had their Coronation," she said.

We all decided to go downstairs and look for a room in which this ceremony may have taken place.

The ballroom was now busy with soldiers moving furniture about in readiness for the wedding. The enormous fireplace was closely examined by all of us but revealed nothing. Several other huge fireplaces in different rooms were investigated – revealing nothing remotely resembling a priest-hole.

John and Alfie were now becoming bored, as was I. I looked at my watch and said, "Just another half an hour then we must go back to Providence House."

Max the soldier came to find us to say that Mrs Davis had made a pot of tea if we had time. I did not think we had time but felt it would be bad mannered to refuse.

In the kitchen Mrs Davis enquired as to what we were looking for and did not seem at all surprised when we answered, "a priest-hole."

"A priest-hole," she repeated, "old Joe Perkins would know where it is. He has done a lot of work up here in his time."

"Where does he live?" asked Max.

"Little Laxlet. Cottage opposite the pub," I said.

"Shall I fetch him?" Max said.

"Yes please," we answered in unison, enjoying our cup of tea.

Circlet of Gold

*

The insignificant looking cupboard was in a small ante-room in the oldest part of The Manor; Joe assured us that this cupboard led to the secret priest-hole. The two shelves were shallow and, as he tilted one, the base and back of the cupboard moved, swinging away to reveal a passage.

We all stared at the space, astounded.

"I'll go in," said Alfie, stepping towards the cupboard.

"No, it could be dangerous," I exclaimed, pulling him back.

"It's a very small passage," said Verity.

"Looks as though it goes behind the fireplace," said Charlie, who now had her head in the cupboard.

"Aye it does that. I'm a bit too old and bent to go in now," said Joe.

"What you need is a rope," said Max who had joined us. "I'll bring one from the truck and a torch."

With the rope tied around his waist, Alfie climbed into the cupboard and turned left into the passage.

"What can you see?" I shouted to him.

"It's a small room," he shouted back.

"Yes, but what can you see?" shouted Verity.

"Nothing. It's empty," he answered.

"Shine the torch everywhere," shouted John.

"I think there's a dead rat in the corner," shouted Alfie, sounding nervous.

"What's the commotion all about?" said Ian, who was now standing behind us and whom we had not heard enter the room.

Feeling rather embarrassed I said, "We're looking for something for Ada, but I'm sorry, if we find it, you can't see it."

"Well Bettina," he said, "Life with Ada is going to be exciting and full of surprises to say the least so I will leave you to your endeavours. Is that Alfie I hear shouting from behind the fireplace?"

"It is Ian. Will it be all right if I explain later?" I said, now feeling quite stressed as John had climbed into the cupboard and was in the priest-hole with Alfie.

Ian left to go to the kitchen to find Mrs Davis and ask her to go with him to his study to discuss the arrangements for catering for the guests who would be staying at The Manor, as well as food for the wedding reception.

Joe Perkins was now enjoying a cup of tea and a piece of Mrs Davis's Christmas cake by the enormous kitchen fire with Esther and Mrs Scribbins and Ian realised he would now need to accustom himself to a rather different lifestyle. One which would include friends calling in, in a rather 'open house' manner, unlike his previous home where there were almost no visitors or friends, unless by appointment. 'Yes, life with Ada is going to be different and wonderful' he thought as he whistled a tune on his way to the study.

"Are you coming out boys?" Charlie said. "You might as well, doesn't look as if there is anything there but a dead rat."

John and Alfie appeared back in the cupboard carrying a brown paper parcel.

"He thought it was a dead rat," said John, "but when I touched it with my foot it's solid."

We closed the door to the room and opened the parcel which contained a fabulous medieval circlet of gold.

Circlet of Gold

"That's the very one," said Verity. "it's just as mam described it, a circlet of gold with stars."

Closing the cupboard beside the fireplace and re-wrapping the circlet we went back into the kitchen.

"Find what you were looking for?" asked Max.

"Yes thank you," I replied giving the rope and torch back to him

"Thank you Joe for helping to find the priest-hole," I said.

"You found it then," he said, looking at the brown paper parcel, then added, "valuable so I'm told. Came from Mesopotamia by all accounts."

"We did Joe." I answered, offering him money for a drink at the pub.

"Suit Ada well, it will. Priceless they do say," he said, adding, "thank you, I'll drink to the bride and groom. Max is taking me home."

Will you be stopping for another cup of tea?" Mrs Scribbins asked.

"No thank you. We've left Agatha on her own. Better get home. See you all soon," I said.

Back at Providence House we took a closer look at the crown which was made of solid gold and truly beautiful. The circlet was plain and attached to it were golden stars, as shining bright and as beautiful as the day the crown was made. I knew Ada would love it.

I would probably now be sewing late into the night but to see Ada wearing her golden crown on her wedding day would make it all worth while.

27

Snow

The first large snowflakes fell about 2pm the day before the wedding. It was dry, serious snow; the kind of snow that builds up, looks beautiful and goes nowhere.

Mrs Davis, with the soldiers from the Doublet Engineers Catering Corps, had their preparations for the reception well under-way. The ballroom at The Manor was now set out with tables and chairs ready for the guests. Mrs Davis had already made the decision to stay the night and was thankful that the wedding cake, made and decorated by her, was safe in the larder next to the butler's pantry. It was to take pride of place in the centre of the top table, to be cut, following the meal, by the bride and groom.

The wedding guests who were staying at The Manor had all arrived by midday on the 28th December. Through Jacobean windows they watched the terrace and deer park becoming a deep winter wonderland of white. The guests were mostly family but also staying were a Major Oldroyd and his wife, both close friends of Ian. Major Oldroyd was the senior officer currently stationed at Little Laxlet army garrison or 'the army camp' as it was known locally.

I had woken up on the morning of Tuesday 29th December, 1936 to silence; the silence which only a blanket of snow can create.

Seven am was early to have breakfast but we gathered

around the table in our warm kitchen at Providence House to discuss the dilemma we now found ourselves in.

"Good job the cars are in the garage," Charlie said.

"I've tried the phone and it's dead. The lines must be down," said Agatha, adding, "I hope the council have started clearing the roads."

"We've measured the snow and it's deeeeep," stated Alfie, adding, "we nearly lost Pip and Logan, they were up to their armpits."

"Deep it most certainly is," said John seriously, "Three feet in places, I should think the roads will be blocked."

"Aye and that's not accountin for t' drifts," added Verity.

"Sounds as though we could be marooned. I'm sure we'll think of something," I said without much confidence.

"Finish up then lads and we'll start shifting some of that snow. We've got a wedding to go to," said Charlie in a positive manner.

"I'll give a hand. I'm well used to snow clearing," said Verity.

By 10am they had the drive from the garage to the road cleared and Charlie was checking the cars.

"I've turned 'em ower so they should be good once the engines warm up," she said, coming into the kitchen and adding, "by the 'eck I'm not 'arf ready for that hot cuppa tea."

A roaring sound outside caused us all to fall silent then rush to look out of the landing window.

An army bulldozer with tracks like a tank and a snow plough attached to its front was clearing the road. It stopped outside Providence House and I opened the window.

A soldier leaned out of the vehicle and shouted up, "The road from The Manor to Little Laxlet is now open and we are now going to clear the road from here to Burside then the track up to Rookery Farm. Can't have the bride late for her wedding."

The army bulldozer then slowly proceeded out of the village.

Snow clearance by the army is not unusual in military situations but Major Oldroyd understood the importance of clearing the roads for the wedding. He had attempted to telephone the council office with no result as the telephone line was dead. He then instructed two soldiers from the catering corps to go in their high, four wheel, flat bed truck over to the army base and give his written instructions to the officer in charge to clear the route to the church. The council would eventually have snow ploughs out clearing the roads, but this was unlikely to be in time for Ada to get to Saint Luke's for 1pm.

At 10:30am Ralph arrived at Providence House with Delicia who came straight into the warm kitchen. Ralph kept the engine running then immediately went back to The Manor to be with Jude.

Delicia, Verity and I changed into our bridesmaid's dresses and royal blue velvet capes. Agatha had made us head dresses of tiny lace flowers on a royal blue velvet headband. By noon we decided to make a start on what would be a slow car journey. With the circlet of gold now carefully packed in a bag, we wore snow boots and carried our shoes in case we needed to leave the car and walk.

Once inside the car I handed a warmed blanket each to Delicia and Verity then, wrapping one around my shoulders, tentatively, started the drive to Burside.

"Pip and Logan will be cosy in the kitchen," I said, to

steady my nerves as I had never driven the car in such conditions.

"They will that," said Verity.

"I'm sure the boys will be good for Agatha. Charlie is an excellent driver," I said.

"They will and she is. The boys will be fine," said Delicia who understood how responsible I felt for John and Alfie.

Passing the end of the track up to Rookery Farm we could hear the army bulldozer-snow plough working hard to clear the snow.

I drove slowly and cautiously, arriving at Burside Parish Church at 12:30pm.

The Vicar invited us into his vestry where, over a small electric fire, we warmed our hands and bridesmaids shoes before putting them on.

Stan and Phyllis arrived with our bouquets, saying what a nightmare of a journey they'd had from Ransington. They had Ada's bouquet with them as the track to the farm had been too risky to attempt in the van but they had managed to drop the button holes and corsages off at The Manor. Mr and Mrs Smith's button hole and corsage were in the box with Ada's bouquet.

The guests, mostly dressed in furs and great coats, began to arrive. Ian, looking splendid in his kilt and black Argyll jacket made a handsome groom; as did Angus, his best man.

Realising that I had not introduced Verity to Ian when we were looking for the crown I did so now, then said, "Come on then girls, we'll go and wait for Ada."

The church was full, the organist gently played, winter sun streamed in through the circular window – but there was no sign of the bride.

"The weather's closing in again," said Verity, as the wind picked up and large snowflakes began to fall. Wrapping our blankets close around our shoulders we stepped from the porch back into the body of the church. The organist kept repeating his repertoire as if on a loop, the guests started chatting amongst themselves and the groom and best man sat waiting in the front pew.

I kept popping to the door to look out at the blizzard and eventually, through the snow, saw the lights of a vehicle which was arriving slowly, in due course stopping as close to the church gate as it could.

Mr Smith was the first to alight from the bulldozer, carrying two boxes and helped by a soldier. Ada, in her full bridal attire, minus the veil, but wearing her mother's fur coat and snow boots, emerged through the blizzard. She was carried along the church path by two soldiers who had joined arms to make a chair lift.

The rest of the wedding party from Rookery Farm alighted from the four wheel drive flat bed army truck.

The church clock struck 2 o'clock.

"Is Ian still here?" Ada asked.

"Yes," I said, helping her to remove her snow boots and her mother's fur coat.

"That's a fucking relief," she said, stepping into her wedding shoes.

We pinned her head-dress and veil in place and smoothed out the front of her wedding gown. Verity and Delicia arranged the train whilst I powdered Ada's nose and she refreshed her lipstick. The snowflakes in Ada's hair had melted and she looked radiant.

Then I showed Ada the circlet of gold and, for probably

the first time in her life, she was momentarily lost for words. I placed the medieval crown on her head, where it nestled into the wax orange blossom and tulle headdress, she then murmured quietly, "Miracles do happen."

"Ready then?" I asked, handing her an enormous bouquet of orchids, white hyacinths, miniature narcissus and lily-of-the-valley all arranged in masses of asparagus fern which trailed almost to the hem of her dress.

The organ began to play Wagner's 'Bridal Chorus', the guests rose from their seats and Ada, on the arm of her father, walked slowly up the aisle to meet her groom.

The wedding service was lovely and I noticed that Ian and Ada looked at each other throughout. One disappointment for me, however, was that Adam had not arrived; 'this is getting to be a habit' I thought.

Mendelsson's wedding march accompanied the wedding party out of the church where it had stopped snowing and the sun was shining.

Ada and Ian left for The Manor in his chauffeur driven Rolls Royce, followed by Ralph in his Riley Nine Lynx with Delicia and Jude.

Verity accompanied me as I drove my little Morris Minor on the snow covered roads back to Little Laxlet.

"We'll just call in at Providence House to check on the dogs and let them stretch their legs in the garden before we go to The Manor," I said.

A stationary car which I did not recognise was parked at the side of the house. Two men were getting out as they saw us approach, which caused me to feel anxious until I realised that one was Duncan the driver and the other was Adam.

I parked my car and we ran towards each other then held each other close.

Going into the kitchen Pip and Logan welcomed us as though I'd been gone for a month.

"Adam, this is Verity," I said.

"We've had a journey and a half," Adam said, "so many blocked roads."

"I'm amazed you've even made it and relieved you are safe," I said, letting the dogs into the garden.

"They won't be long in this weather then we must go straight to The Manor," I said.

"I know, Duncan will run us up there, then he's heading for home," Adam said.

The menu at the reception was wonderful. Mrs Davis and the boys of the catering corps had excelled themselves with the food.

Leek and Potato Soup

Roast Chicken and Turkey
Roast Potatoes
Winter Vegetables

Pear Belle Helen
(Which Ada knew was a favourite of Delicia and Ralph)

Wedding Cake

Unfortunately the band did not arrive as their van broke down in the snow. However a band from the garrison quickly replaced them and soon Ada and Ian were dancing their first dance together as husband and wife.

'It Had To Be You' was the music they chose and, as I looked at them, obviously so happy together I thought, 'good choice.'

Adam took me in his arms and it was wonderful.

"It's a foxtrot," he said.

"I know, our favourite," I murmured, suddenly feeling tired after such an eventful day.

"Are you organised for our holiday?" Adam asked.

With everything that had happened over the last week the holiday was the last thing on my mind, so I wasn't at all organised, but replied, "Yes of course I am. Where are we going?"

"Surprise," he said. "That's all I'm saying, we leave at noon tomorrow and please don't forget the passports."

He looked happy and I was delighted to be in his arms dancing to 'It Had To Be You'. Noon tomorrow seemed a long way off.

28

The Holiday

I **was awake before** daylight on December 30th 1936, my clock read 6am. Unsure what to take for this surprise holiday I selected a variety of clothing for myself and the boys; all then packed into three suitcases.

By noon we were excited and ready. The passports, still in my documents case, were now safely in my handbag and we were waiting in the hall at Providence House.

The weather was extremely cold and much snow still lay on the roads, but I was assured by the wireless that the forecast was good.

A car horn tooted, so we said good bye to Agatha, Charlie, Verity and the dogs.

Pulling my coat tightly around me and ensuring the boys had theirs buttoned up we headed down the path to the car.

Duncan the driver was in the car, but there was no sign of Adam.

"Climb in," Duncan said, stowing our suitcases in the boot.

"Where's Adam?" I asked, as we drove out of Little Laxlet.

"Gone on ahead, he took an earlier train," Duncan answered.

"What do you mean, gone on ahead? Gone on ahead – to where?" I asked with a touch of exasperation in my voice.

"I don't rightly know. Something to do with work. Says

he'll meet you there," Duncan said.

"Where?" I asked, feeling frustration building up.

"All I know is to give you the train tickets," he said calmly.

I felt concerned, unlike John and Alfie who enjoyed the intrigue and were speculating as to where the train tickets would take us.

As we alighted from the car at Ransington railway station Duncan handed me an envelope containing the tickets saying, "Platform 2. You're catching the 13:56 to Kings Cross. Then take a taxi to the Dorchester Hotel. There's money in the envelope for the taxi.

I took the envelope.

"Oh! Nearly forgot, here's a picnic for the three of you," Duncan said, adding, "Mrs Davis packed it for you this morning."

"Mrs Davis?" I queried, thinking 'this is getting stranger.'

"Brilliant breakfast she made us this morning at The Manor," Duncan said, "she said to tell you to have a good holiday."

John and Alfie, both fans of the wireless programme 'Dick Barton – Special Agent' were now speculating as to whether Duncan might be a special agent.

We bought comics and magazines from the news-stand in the railway station and then boarded the 13:56 to London.

The tickets were for reserved seats in a first class carriage which was warm as well as comfortable; I must have dozed off to sleep for a while. The boys engrossed themselves in their comics and when I awoke we ate our delicious picnic. The journey was straightforward, I read my magazine and completed the crossword on the back page.I felt totally relaxed now and wondered occasionally where Ian had taken

Ada for their honeymoon and if she had remembered to pack her black and red cami-knickers.

The London traffic was incredibly busy as we took our taxi drive to the Dorchester Hotel.

"A holiday in London. The lads at school will never believe it," John said in an excited voice.

"Are we going to see Buckingham Palace?" asked Alfie.

"I'd rather see the Houses of Parliament," said John.

"Well, it all depends on how long we are staying, Adam didn't say," I said.

It was now so dark that only the street lights and the lights of the traffic could be seen.

The Dorchester Hotel was huge and seemed exceptionally grand as we entered.

'How was it I always revert to type; that of 'country bumpkin', when in lavish surroundings', I thought.

We tentatively approached the highly polished reception desk.

"How may I help you?" asked the smiling receptionist who looked elegant, confident and sophisticated.

"I believe there is a room booked for me," I said, adding, "Miss Dawson."

She consulted the register.

"Yes Miss Dawson, it's a family room for you and your brothers. The porter will look after your luggage," she said, handing me a big key with room number 62 on it's shiny brass tab, simultaneously summoning the porter with no more than a glance in his direction.

"Oh Miss Dawson, this envelope is for you," she said, handing me a manilla envelope.

"Thank you," I said, then followed the porter to the lift.

Room 62 was incredibly spacious with three beds, sofas and enormous windows encased in swag curtains. The hotel porter, in full uniform, had transported our cases on a brass trolley and I felt anxious as I knew I needed to give him a tip. I'd seen hotel guests tipping porters in the Hollywood movies at the pictures, but how much to give him, that I did not know.

'If only Adam were here', I thought, giving the man 2/- and hoping that was the correct amount.

"This is a bit posh!" John exclaimed.

"It is," I agreed, "but where on earth Adam is, well that is a mystery!"

I sat on a comfortable sofa and opened the envelope, inside which there was a note.

My Darling Bettina,

If you are reading this then you and the boys will be at the Dorchester. I hope your room is comfortable.
Please have dinner tonight and breakfast in the morning.
Don't worry about paying as I have an account with the hotel. The cost of your meals will go onto it, as will the bill for your room.
My work seems to have taken over and I have several things to complete before tomorrow.
Enjoy dinner and breakfast, I will meet you in the hotel foyer at 10am in the morning.
I promise that I will then be officially on holiday and you will have my undivided attention.

I love you my darling.

Adam. xxx

ps Please have all your luggage with you.

'Undivided attention, well that'll be a first!' I thought, feeling slightly piqued.

I explained the contents of Adam's note to John and Alfie. They both agreed that a holiday in The Dorchester would be acceptable if they could see the London sights.

"I don't think we will be staying here for more than one night," I said to them, "Adam's ps says to have our luggage with us in the morning."

"Very strange Mr Watson," Alfie said.

"Stranger by the minute Mr Holmes," added John.

I could only agree.

As promised, Adam was waiting in the hotel foyer at 10am the following morning. I handed the room key to the receptionist who suddenly did not seem so intimidating. Walking towards Adam my heart swelled with love for him. The boys were already by his side and visibly excited.

"The holiday starts now," said John as Adam kissed me on both cheeks and we hugged.

"He won't tell us where we are going," said Alfie, "and I really, really, *really* need to know.

"Victoria please," Adam said to the driver of the black cab.

"Going somewhere nice sir?" the driver asked.

"I hope so," said Adam, sliding closed the small glass partition between driver and passengers.

We then travelled by train from Victoria to Southampton then by taxi to the port.

The ship was both enormous and stately.

'Some holiday this is going to be,' I thought as we boarded The Queen Mary.

"Where are we going?" I asked Adam.

"We are going to New York by the southern route," Adam answered, obviously imparting information to us on a need to know basis.

"New York," I said, feeling quite flabbergasted and glad I'd remembered to bring the passports.

"Yes New York, and you my darling are not going to lift a finger for the entire holiday," he said.

'Not lift a finger, I like the sound of that,' I thought as we were shown to our suite of rooms.

29

Friendship

As the ship was about to depart from Southampton we all went on deck. Crowds had gathered on the dock side and a band played traditional jazz music. Those of us on board waved and threw streamers to the onlookers below. We didn't know anyone in the crowd but we waved regardless; the atmosphere was most definitely upbeat and joyous.

There were three prolonged, loud blasts of the ship's horn and our journey began.

The Queen Mary was positively sumptuous with many lavishly decorated rooms often in the Art Deco style. In the dining room our journey could be tracked by a small crystal copy of the ship travelling across a huge decorative map of the North Atlantic Ocean. Two routes were depicted; we were travelling by the southern route to avoid icebergs.

When Adam, the boys and I went to the dining room for dinner that first night of the voyage we were seated at a large table set for eleven diners. Adam ordered three bottles of champagne which were brought to our table in a huge ice-bucket. A jug of lemonade and one of water were also placed on the table. I began to be curious as to who the other diners might be.

Ralph, Delicia and aunt Eliza Jane joined us, followed by Ada and Ian with his boys. My surprise, as they sat down, was utterly genuine as my open mouth must have indicated. It was wonderful to see my aunt and my friends and I was amazed how well the secret had been kept. Then I remembered that Ian had not told Ada about the surprise honeymoon; had she known I doubted she would have been able to keep the secret and would have let it slip into conversation.

"How wonderful to see you all," I said, then asking, "where's Jude?"

"We brought his nanny along to make life easier. Jude is in bed now, it's been a hectic couple of days," said Ralph.

"We stayed at the Ritz last night," Ada said, "Ian never said a word about today and going to America."

"Well you did say the honeymoon was to be a surprise," I said, thinking how happy they looked.

"Did you stay in London last night?" I asked Delicia and Ralph.

"Yes, we stayed at the town house with Quentin and Arjana," Delicia answered.

"Still the same girlfriend then?" I said.

"Yes she's very much in evidence," Ralph said.

"Charming girl," aunt Eliza Jane said, "introduced me to the cocktail 'French 75'. We partook of several, delightful evening, delightful"

The sommelier had opened the champagne and our glasses were full. Adam stood up and said, *"A toast to friendship."*

We clinked our glasses and echoed the toast.

Ralph made the second toast which was, *"A toast to surprises"* which we all repeated whilst clinking our glasses.

Ian made the third toast, *"To honeymoons and holidays"* clinking our glasses again we dittoed his sentiments.

As we ended our dinner, which was probably the best food I've ever tasted, Adam said to John and Alfie, "Boys, I need to have a chat with Bettina on our own. It will only take a little while. Do you think you could explore the ship – say for half an hour?

"What a good idea," Ian and Ralph said in unison.

Ian then said, "Edwin and Seth said they want to explore so we can all go together."

The four boys then went off with Ian and Ralph to explore.

Declicia said she would go and check on Jude and the nanny.

Aunt Eliza said she was tired and needed an early night.

Ada then said, "I'm fucking cream-crackered, I'm going for a lie down."

I was starting to feel suspicious!

Back in our suite of rooms Adam looked serious, which made me feel concerned.

"Sit down Bettina," he said, "I have a few things to tell you."

The bed looked inviting but I chose to sit on a chair. Adam moved another chair and sat directly facing me.

'This must be important, hope it won't ruin the holiday.' I couldn't help thinking.

"I don't quite know where to start," Adam said earnestly, "but I need to tell you this tonight."

I didn't say a word.

"It's about my job," he said.

"Your job with Nick Van der Linden?" I said.

"Well in a way. I do, of course, have a job with Nick as you know," Adam said.

I sat quietly.

"But I have another job," he said.

'Two jobs', I thought, 'it's no wonder I never see you.'

"Well you know I've been in Germany and France lately," he said.

"Yes," I said, "something to do with Nick's printing presses."

"That is true, I ordered two in Heidelberg to be sent to America," he said, adding, "my other job is with the British government."

"You mean you're a SPY! I exclaimed.

"Not exactly, more an agent. I gather information," Adam said.

"What kind of information?" was my next question.

"Obviously I can't say too much but my opinion is that within two or three years we will be at war with Germany. Hitler is a powerful, sabre rattling dictator. The situation is deteriorating there for ordinary people even though they don't see it, apart from the Jewish population. The Nazis cannot be allowed to continue and Britain will, I'm sure intervene."

I said nothing but took his hands in mine.

Adam then said, "My boss, the Foreign Minister, has given me permission to tell you this as it is only fair that you understand my sudden absences. I work in the shadows for our government. My job with Nick, although genuine, is a cover."

This was a huge piece of information for me to take in and we just sat there for a while.

Then I said, "But they said the Great War was the war to end all wars."

"I know my darling but they hadn't bargained for *Führer Hitler*," Adam said quietly.

"Yes," I said, "I only know what I read in the papers or see on the Pathé News and he does seem scary. Though the débutantes are still going to Germany and Austria to meet eligible young men and party."

"From what I've seen this is true and some have become Nazi sympathisers," Adam said.

"WHAT! British girls?" was my shocked response.

"Yes," he affirmed.

"That is truly shocking," I said.

Adam then said, "I have told you as much as I'm allowed. How are you feeling?"

"Worried. Concerned for your safety. All those kinds of things," I replied.

"Do I have your word on secrecy and security?" Adam asked.

"Of course you do Adam. I just want you to be safe. The thought of war is very frightening," was my heartfelt response.

"Then we must never again speak about the conversation we have just had. Most agents, and there are only a few of us, don't tell their fiancées but I had to as I knew you would suss me out," he said.

"Too right, I would," I said, then we moved together and lay on the bed.

The kiss which followed that most serious of serious conversations, was tender, caring and warm. We held each other close and although we were both fully dressed our arms and legs became entwined. My love for Adam was so great I dared not even think about the consequences of war. I decided not to allow Adam's disclosure to spoil the holiday but to just enjoy being in his arms which I was for about ten minutes.

"I have some news for you Miss Dawson," Adam said, sitting up.

"What?" I asked.

"We are getting married," he said.

"Yes I know, in May," was my response.

"No not in May but tomorrow," he said.

"Tomorrow," I repeated, "How?"

"Tomorrow is the first day of 1937 and the Captain of this ship will marry us. It's all arranged," Adam said in a voice which I knew could not be argued with.

"Is that legal?" I asked.

"Well almost," he replied, looking a bit sheepish.

"What do you mean, almost? It either is or it isn't," I said.

"Bettina you drive me crazy," he said with mild frustration beginning to show. " for once in your life allow others to look after you – please."

I realised that this was a fait accompli so it would be useless to argue.

Adam explained, "The ceremony will be on the bridge of this ship at 3pm, performed by the ship's captain and blessed by the pastor. When we arrive in New York we take the marriage documents to the Court House and a judge will perform a civil ceremony lasting only a few minutes. It's all arranged and you are over twenty one although I do believe the age of consent in America is eighteen."

"Ah," I said.

"Ah. What do you mean, Ah," he said.

"Well I'm not twenty one," I said, thinking, 'time to lay all my cards on the table'.

"Of course you're twenty one, it was your twenty first in November," he said.

I took my birth certificate out of my document case. My date of birth clearly stated 16th November, 1916 which meant that I was now twenty, not twenty one.

An explanation was obviously required for what I considered to be a mere oversight but clearly Adam felt it was of importance.

"When I was at school," I said, "It was a small country school and we were not streamed in years but in groups; I was always with the older girls. It became easy to just add a year on to my age to be the same as them and no one ever questioned it. When mam died and I took over responsibility for the boys I just kept the added year there. Made it easier for dealing with their school and such like. I did give my proper age for the driving licence and passport though. That's it, so if you don't want to marry me now then just say."

"Of course I want to marry you my beautiful Bettina and tomorrow it is," Adam said, laughing at my sad face.

"But what will I wear," I said, realising that tomorrow would be my wedding day and I was totally unprepared.

"Don't worry Delicia and Ada have your outfit all organised," Adam said.

"You mean they've known all along?" I exclaimed.

"Yes, and they kept the secret well," he said, smiling and taking me into his arms again.

'Ada has kept a secret – then miracles do happen.' I thought.

"Shall we go and tell them you now know?" Adam asked.

"Delicia and Ada have probably gone to bed," I said.

"Don't think so, it's New Year's Eve, remember," Adam replied.

30

New York

Following the New Year's Eve party, which went on until the early hours, everyone slept late on New Year's Day.

About 1pm Ada, Delicia and aunt Eliza Jane called to help me prepare for the wedding.

Eliza Jane had shortened Delicia's Norman Hartnell wedding gown which now fitted me perfectly. Ada had brought her gold bridal crown in the box with the Carrickmacross lace wedding veil.

Aunt Eliza Jane made herself comfortable on the large chaise longue.

"Have a bath," said Ada, "it'll calm your nerves."

"I don't have any nerves," I said.

"Well it might relax you," Delicia said, running the bath.

I certainly was feeling rather tense, not being used to surprises and not being in control.

The bath was luxurious, perfumed with bubbles, courtesy of the Cunard-White Star shipping line. I sank into it.

"There, that's better," said Ada, handing me a glass of champagne and then sitting in the Lloyd Loom bathroom chair.

Delicia brought in a stool from the bedroom which she sat on saying, "Aunt Eliza is having a doze."

They both sat there looking at me in the bath.

"Where are John and Alfie?" I asked.

"With Seth and Edwin and they are fine," Delicia said.

"Agatha sent you this," Ada said, handing me a small package.

"Agatha!" I exclaimed. "you mean Agatha knew about this."

The package contained a pale blue hand made lace garter.

"This, as you call it, has been the best kept secret ever," Delicia said.

"Well you've got your old, your borrowed and blue all you need now is your something new," Ada said, exchanging a conspiratorial glance with Delicia, then adding. "Out of the bath now, we don't want Adam thinking he's marrying a fucking prune."

'I can always rely on Ada to keep me in the moment'. I thought, wrapping myself in a huge, fluffy bath towel.

A box wrapped in silver tissue sat on the dressing table. Inside was a pair of diamond earrings with a pear shaped pearl hanging from each cluster of diamonds. The card read. *'I love you'*. My something new was this wedding gift from Adam.

"I know just what you are thinking Bettina," Delicia said.

"Do you?" I said.

"Course she does and so do I, That's why we got these," Ada said, handing me a small box.

The gold cuff links, engraved AR were the perfect wedding gift for Adam from me.

"I'll take these along to Adam," Delicia said, "We'll change then come back to help you into your dress."

The Norman Hartnell wedding gown fitted me perfectly. Ada and Delicia secured, then arranged the Carrickmacross

Circlet of Gold

lace veil around my face and shoulders and I couldn't quite believe that I was the bride and about to be married. Great aunt Eliza Jane placed the circlet of golden stars on my red-brown hair which I had decided to wear in a French pleat.

"You look fabulous!" Ada and Delicia said together.

"Gorgeous just gorgeous," said aunt Eliza Jane, dabbing her eyes with her lace edged handkerchief.

A knock on the bedroom door, which then opened brought John and Alfie into the room.

"We have your your flowers," John said, handing me a bouquet of cream roses.

"Thank you," I said, "You are both looking as smart as I've ever seen you."

"And you look as beautiful as I've ever seen you," Alfie said.

Delicia clicked her camera taking photographs which would, forever, remind us of such a special day.

"Who is giving you away?" Ada asked.

I looked at John and Alfie. "My two boys of course," I said, "Will you both give me away?"

"We certainly will if it means you'll ease off the rein," Alfie said, laughing.

"It's a deal," I said.

"Bet she doesn't," said John.

"Come on then, let's go, Adam will be waiting," Aunt Eliza Jane said.

*

Arriving in New York was exciting if extremely cold. I was now Bettina Rutherford and as we sailed past the Statue of Liberty my thoughts were of my love for Adam and our one week honeymoon in a suite at the Plaza Hotel before our return to England on The Queen Mary.

John, Alfie, Seth and Edwin would be staying with aunt Eliza Jane, Delicia, Ralph and Jude and his nanny, at the Van der Linden's residence out at the Hamptons.

'Quite a houseful.' I thought, but there had been a conversation about ice skating and skiing.

Ada and Ian would be honeymooning at the Waldorf Hotel.

On the third day of our stay in New York in January 1937, Adam and I went to the Court House where a Judge performed a short civil ceremony, legalising our marriage. Aunt Eliza Jane, Ada and Delicia joined us and stood as our witnesses.

The Honeymoon

Dear reader, I know you must be wondering about Bettina and Adam and their week honeymooning at the Plaza Hotel, in a suite overlooking Central Park, New York.

The word I would use to describe our honeymoon would be sublime.

Yes, sublime is the perfect word.

About the Author

Now enjoying retirement, Hettie lives in Buckinghamshire with her husband and two cats. Much of her time is devoted to her related passions of sewing, quilting and social history.

In her working years she developed an interest in the barriers women faced in all aspects of life, particularly related to health, family and work.

Hettie has been heartened to witness, in recent decades, the widening opportunities for women, although life/work balance continues to be tricky for most.

In her own career she has helped to support families as a nurse, midwife and health visitor.

Hettie's first two books, *Threads of Steel* and *Little Bronze Girl* have now been expanded in this sequel *Circlet of Gold*, completing the trilogy.

The importance of female friendships and good humour are illustrated throughout the story.

Finally, Hettie has appreciated the many kind comments from the readers of *Threads of Steel* and *Little Bronze Girl* and hopes that *Circlet of Gold* brings pleasure and enjoyment to all who read it.

Lightning Source UK Ltd.
Milton Keynes UK
UKHW021547080221
378428UK00010B/2405